DEFENDER

THE VIGILANTE CHRONICLES™ BOOK SIX

NATALIE GREY

MICHAEL ANDERLE

L M B P N

DISRUPTIVE IMAGINATION®

THE DEFENDER TEAM

Thanks to our JIT Readers

Mary Morris
Danika Fedeli
Peter Manis
John Ashmore
Keith Verret
Diane L. Smith
Angel LaVey
Daniel Weigert
Kelly Ethan
Tracey Byrnes

If We've missed anyone, please let us know!

Editor
Lynne Stiegler

From Natalie

For M and T

From Michael

To Family, Friends and
Those Who Love
To Read.
May We All Enjoy Grace
To Live The Life We Are
Called.

CHAPTER ONE

There were a number of high-tech strategies available to someone who was hoping to avoid surveillance.

After all, for a Jotun, surveillance and sabotage were not merely possible, but true dangers. To participate in day-to-day life with other species, a Jotun must wear a mechanical suit fitted with a central tank that would hold the Jotun's jellyfish-like body. They used the suits like others would use their bodies, but those in higher-end and more specialized suits were also able to send and receive messages, use weapons embedded in the suits, and scan people, machines, and objects.

This made the suits vulnerable. The Jotun government had extensive protocols in place to keep matters of state from being spied upon. Otherwise, the suits could be hacked to send all speech to a third party, or make the weapons malfunction, or track the Jotun's movement.

The Jotuns had, of necessity, evolved some of the most complex computer systems in this sector. Very few other species posed a true threat to them in that regard, it was mostly their own homegrown hackers and vigilantes that they feared.

When Jeltor went back to Jotuna, therefore, seeking out the top brass of the Navy to help him expose the Senate's latest treason, he spent a good deal of time trying to figure out how to escape surveillance.

Admiral Jeqwar chose an option he would never have anticipated: she found several old, discarded biosuits and cleaned them up just enough to be habitable. They were so old that their computers barely functioned beyond providing life support. Hacking them would be an exercise in frustration, and it was unlikely that any of the Senate's hackers even *knew* the programming languages these suits ran on.

Jeltor admired the admiral's plan, but the suits were damned uncomfortable. He was used to his own suit, which he had modified extensively over the years. Without scanners, communications capabilities, or weapons, he felt naked.

Also, cold. This suit did not calibrate temperature the same way his did.

He bobbed in the water uncomfortably as they walked toward the waterfront. Some of the admiral's aides were trailing after them, and Jeltor was sure that there were more who were keeping watch, protecting these two revolutionaries.

Jeltor would never have guessed in his youth that the term "revolutionary" would apply to him. He'd joined the Navy when he was young, progressing through the ranks as his mind would allow; Jotun Naval captains each controlled an entire ship during battle, and very few had the mental capacity to control the largest ships. Only a handful in each generation were able to be admirals, who could control an entire fleet.

He had served well once he graduated, becoming known for being decisive and fair, a good captain to the crews that ran his ships when they were not in a battle. He had known about the corruption in the Senate, of course, because everyone knew about it, but he'd had a youthful belief that corruption was inevitable in any civilized species.

In any case, his younger self had thought the Jotuns were better than other species. They should not worry about corruption as long as it did not cost them territories or good trade deals.

Jeltor wanted to slap his younger self for having such insular, ignorant notions. He had first realized some of his errors when he began to interact with other species and found them to be not the brutish savages he'd been told, but intelligent—and even dangerous. This gradual awakening had made him start questioning everything, whether he wanted to or not.

The final straw had come when he was taken hostage by pirates. Rescued by a human named Barnabas, Jeltor had learned the Yennai Corporation, which had infiltrated the Jotun government and was seeking to become the dominant power in the entire sector. Far from fighting it, the Jotun Senate was allowing this and looking the other way. Jeltor had been accused of treason for standing against the Yennai Corporation.

He hadn't *wanted* to be a revolutionary. He'd simply

stood for what was right, and somehow that had made him one.

Now he spent his time looking over his shoulder for assassins and worrying about surveillance. It seemed like a nightmare, something that would happen to someone else. Unfortunately, it was all too real.

"So," Admiral Jeqwar said when they reached the waterfront. "Why did you need to meet?"

"Have you ever heard of the Infrastructure Revitalization Committee?" Jeltor asked her.

She turned her biosuit to look at him. "No," she said cautiously. "But it must be more important than it sounds if you're here to talk to me about it."

Jeltor gave a little laugh. "I've been thinking the same thing. Unfortunately, I don't know what it is. It was a tip given to us by…well, I don't know that, either."

"So you came here to tell me that you've received a tip that could mean anything from an anonymous source?"

"Not exactly anonymous." Jeltor wiggled his tentacles somewhat nervously. "I trust I can say the following in confidence?"

"Yes," she said wryly. "We're already under suspicion of treason, and we've indubitably committed mutiny. Let's not get worried about rule-breaking now."

Despite himself, Jeltor laughed. He had always been a bit in awe of Admiral Jeqwar. She was a legend, and her reputation was well-earned. What he had not expected, when he became part of the resistance against the Jotun Senate, was that she would be forthright and no-nonsense. The Jotuns who could be admirals were so rare and so intelligent that he had assumed she would be very cold and superior, looking down on everyone else.

None of them were like that, it turned out. They were very practical, and had no patience for bullshit. It made Jeltor feel better about the fact that they had led the Navy into mutiny. If he was on their side, he felt he was on the right side.

He was worried that his latest mission, however, might concern even them.

"How much do you *know* of Huword's death?" he asked.

She gave him an annoyed glance. "Very little, as well you should know. No one's said a damned thing."

"Huword was a traitor," Jeltor said bluntly. "He was working for the Senate, not only during the mutiny but for other purposes that we don't even understand yet." He hated to tell her the truth. Huword had been well-liked.

Despite her practicality, she could not seem to believe this. "*Huword?*" she asked him bluntly. "Of all people, *him?*"

"I know." Jeltor felt a deep pang of sadness. He had believed that Huword was his friend. "I know," he repeated, "but it's true. He was working for the Senate, and whatever he was doing, it's involved—somehow—with the committee I mentioned. And *that* was why he was assassinated."

The admiral was no fool. "If you know only parts of this," she said slowly, "then you clearly weren't the one who assassinated him."

"You thought I was?" It was grimly amusing to find out he'd become so infamous that people thought he was off performing vigilante justice, assassinating his fellow Naval captains.

"Our intelligence suggested you were involved some-how." She gave the ripple that was the Jotun equivalent of a shrug.

"Only after the fact. Barnabas was the one who found out about the murder."

"Humans again." Her suit shook its head. "If I'm honest, I don't like another species being quite so involved in our business."

Jeltor knew better than to take this as a reprimand. Indeed, he understood it for what it was: a confidence. Jotuns were told from an early age that they were superior to all other species and that they were the lone beacon of true civilization in the sector.

Even once you realized that was false, it was difficult to undo the years of belief.

"I think whoever ordered Huword's assassination feels the same," Jeltor told her. "They tried to warn us off. I think the assassin acted without their knowledge when they told us about the committee. We ran into them again when..." He rippled again, worriedly. "When we killed Senator Biset."

The admiral muttered a quiet oath. "You killed a *senator?*"

"That wasn't what we thought we were—" He broke off. Excuses were useless. "Yes," he said simply. Then, because she was still staring at him, he explained succinctly, "They set a trap for us on Gokrun III, and we managed to get out of it. The assassin helped us kill them; it was the only way to get out of the trap. Then they told us about the committee and left."

The admiral stared out over the waterfront and said

nothing for a long moment.

Hevarod, the capital city of Jotuna, had originally been constructed underwater but had been moved as the Jotuns began developing and testing biosuits. It was now along the coastline of Jotuna's largest island, and there was a portion of the metropolis that was suitable for aliens. The official business of the government was even conducted in buildings aliens could access, but there were always calls to move things into the ocean and force aliens to wear biosuits to survive there.

"You want us to help you look for this committee," the admiral said finally. She sounded weary. "I'll be honest with you, Captain—I do not like learning of all the things my government has done. I do not like it at all."

Jeltor nodded. There was nothing to say. He agreed fully with the sentiment. None of them wanted to know this. They persevered only because if they didn't, they would destroy themselves from within. Never had there been a more reluctant group of revolutionaries, he thought. The idea was bitterly amusing.

"Huword was involved in several attacks," he continued. "They were all on remote colonies, some our own, some along the borders of other species' territories. They were all blamed on pirates. A few of the civilians were found tortured and killed in some instances. The rest vanished. That probably has something to do with this committee."

"*Probably?*"

"The more I learn about Huword, the more I think nothing would surprise me."

"Then it's good he's dead," she said brutally. "Well, this is a mess. We'll look into it. We'll search for anyone who seems to know about it. You'll be interested to learn that Biset's death hasn't been announced. Clearly, someone doesn't want people looking into his work."

"Any instructions for me?" Jeltor asked.

She considered. "See if you can find out who had Huword killed. They don't want any other species to know. Well, if he was abducting civilians, I can see why, but we *need* to know what they know. Find out what you can, and then come to any of the admirals. We know how to get word to one another outside any of the channels others know about."

Jeltor nodded. That was good to know.

He took his leave of her, transferring back to his own biosuit with exquisite relief. With his own weapons and computers, not to mention his custom-heated tank, he was much more—

The attack came so fast that he had no time to react. The EMP blast knocked out his suit's communications and sensory panel for a few critical seconds. As Jeltor reeled, trying to use his own eyes and ears to figure out what was going on, his suit was locked in place, disabled by means he could not see.

He could hear the voices, but barely.

"Is he alive?"

"Yes." There was a pause while Jeltor's suit was tipped, and the whole world went black. Dimly, he heard the second voice say, "Load him onto the ship before anyone sees."

Wherever they'd put him, they must have closed it off, because he heard a door slam and then nothing more. A vehicle of some sort lurched into motion. His suit stayed locked up. With his communications array down, Jeltor struggled in the darkness of his tank.

But it was no use. These people had planned, and planned well.

At least he had gotten word to the admiral. He floated motionless, terror and vengeance swirling in his mind, and came back to that one tiny victory: he had gotten word to the admiral. If they wanted to kill him, he thought, they could—but they could not undo what he had set in train.

It was a mercy of a sort that he did not realize how wrong he was.

CHAPTER TWO

Aliana Waters took a big gulp of beer and shuddered. Beer had only just started being drunk beyond Federation territory, and although it was a popular drink, the process of making it hadn't exactly been perfected by its new fans.

The rules for beer, therefore, were simple: order it in a fit of nostalgia, take a sip, regret your life choices, and chug the rest quickly to avoid tasting it.

She really should have learned better by now, but beer was one of the few things she missed, and she couldn't quite give up on it. She took a deep breath, plugged her nose, and gulped down the rest of her mug, slamming it back on the table when she was done with a look of intense concentration.

The concentration was necessary to keep from bringing it all back up. There was a pungent taste in this beer that the aliens in the room—Yofu and Torcellans, mostly—

seemed to think was delicious, but it reminded Aliana of things that should *definitely* not go in beer.

"Excuse me," said a voice nearby.

Aliana looked up and blinked in surprise. She wasn't sure she'd ever seen this species before. Its body had a shell somewhat like an armadillo's, although it otherwise looked roughly humanoid. Another, slightly smaller armadillo-alien stood to one side of it. If the smaller one were human, Aliana would say it looked long-suffering and annoyed, but she knew better than to treat guesswork as fact when it came to alien emotions.

"Yes?" she asked. She didn't really want to talk to anyone right now, but her mother had always been a stickler for etiquette. The aliens didn't seem to be armed, and they *were* being polite—so Aliana would be, too.

For now.

"May we sit?" asked the first alien.

"Sure, why not." She sat back in her chair as they both sat down. "What are you?" It was a blunt question, but Aliana wasn't up for a long, drawn-out conversation on the topic.

"We are Hieto," said the smaller one. "I am Tik'ta, and this is Zinqued."

"Hi," Aliana said with a nod. Hieto. She'd vaguely heard of them, but she didn't think she'd ever seen one. "I'm Aliana."

"We know," said the one known as Zinqued. Her implanted scanners told her that it was probably male. "We asked the bartender."

Aliana wrapped her fingers around the now-empty mug and leaned forward, smiling a bit too politely. "And what was so interesting about me that you asked the bartender?"

Tik'ta seemed to sense the threat in those words and looked like she (the scanners again) wanted to leave, but Zinqued didn't seem inclined to go. He shook his head and waved both hands slightly.

"My apologies if I offended, Captain Waters." He pronounced the human title carefully. "That is how I should address you to show respect, yes? My apologies. Humans are rare here, and I have some interest in human matters."

Aliana fought the urge to groan. This was an entire steaming pile of topics she didn't want to touch with a ten-foot pole.

"It's a fine title, but please don't use it again." It was even technically accurate. She had a ship, so she was a captain. The fact that she had no crew and no home, and that her ship was falling apart at the seams, just made it more of a cruel mockery than anything else—even if Zinqued clearly hadn't meant it that way.

He stumbled over a few apologies, which she waved away.

"I'm really not interested in talking about the Federation," she said plainly. "I know it's interesting to everyone out here, but there's a lot of news on the subject, so if you could just read that—"

"Perhaps I should be more specific," the Hieto interrupted. "I do not mean the business of all humans out here in this sector—"

"Good, because we don't have just one set of business."

She tried not to sound too bitter. "It's not like we're all *allies.*"

The two Hieto probably didn't know much about human emotions, but they knew enough not to ask any more questions on this point. A person would have to be a robot not to hear the anger and hurt in her tone.

But Zinqued clearly wasn't intending to be put off. Indeed, he seemed almost intrigued by her admission. He leaned in slightly and asked, "Do you know anything about a human named Barnabas?"

"No." Aliana shook her head wearily. "I don't. If he owes you money, I have zero interest in helping you collect it." No way in hell was she planning to become a debt collector.

"Ah, you misunderstand. He does not so much owe us money," Zinqued spread his hands, "as… Let us say that he has things we want."

This, oddly, seemed to spur Tik'ta from annoyance to outright rebellion. "Zinqued, this is a bad idea."

He shot her a look that clearly meant, "Shut up."

But now Aliana *was* interested. "What's a bad idea?" she asked, not even bothering to hide her knowing look. She was in the reckless sort of bad mood to make very poor decisions, but if someone *else* was going to do so, she could probably settle for just watching. Like a train wreck, she thought contemplatively.

The beer seemed to be kicking in. Some humans were apparently upgraded to the point where they couldn't get drunk anymore, but she wasn't. She just had the standard life-enhancing, good-healing, aren't-we-clever assortment that almost every human out here had.

All that meant, in her opinion, was that she'd survived things she shouldn't and had memories she didn't want. She pitied the ones with even more upgrades. Hers hadn't worked out for her.

She watched Zinqued and Tik'ta and waited. It was that or start a bar fight.

Zinqued considered carefully and then said, "We've had several run-ins with Barnabas, and we're attempting to construct a team to…interact with him again."

"What the fuck does that mean?"

"It means," said Tik'ta, annoyance dripping from her tone, "that Zinqued's tried to steal the *Shinigami* several times, has only survived the attempts by Barnabas' mercy, and he's determined to keep trying."

Aliana looked down into her mug and wished she had more beer. Since she didn't, she settled for asking Tik'ta, "Why are you here, then? You don't seem to think it's a good idea."

"I don't," Tik'ta said bluntly, "but my old captain ran up enough of a record that I can't get hired anywhere good, and if I leave *this* idiot—" she jerked her head at Zinqued "he'll get himself killed in a week." To Zinqued, she said, "She doesn't know anything about him. She won't help you."

"I didn't say *that*," Aliana said recklessly.

Zinqued, who had started to stand with a defeated expression, looked almost hopeful.

Tik'ta sighed. "What?" she asked, like someone who really hoped she'd misheard.

"You want to steal a ship?" Aliana asked. "That sounds fun." Hell, if they could teach her how to steal ships, maybe she could get hers back. Not the bucket of bolts she presently owned, of course. That was only her ship in terms of legality.

No, *her* ship, her *actual* ship. She wanted her damned ship back, and this chance encounter was showing that she'd been going about it all wrong. Lawrence had made it all nice and neat on paper, so there was no getting it back without him selling it, and he'd just *love* to charge her way too much. He'd cleaned her out, too, bank accounts and all.

Aliana had thought she was finished. She'd been taking courier jobs and patching her ship with scrap metal and glue.

But if she could *steal* the ship back from Lawrence...

Yeah, she liked this plan more every second. She grinned at the two Hieto. "Here's the deal: you teach me how to steal ships, I help you steal this human's ship, and then *you* help *me* steal a ship."

Both Hieto sat back down. They were, she noticed, looking at her like she was insane. She didn't care, though. This was the happiest she'd been in months. She had something warm and tantalizing in her chest that felt very much like hope. A small part of her told her that hope was dangerous and likely to clobber her on the way out, but she was tired of being so damned sad all the time.

She'd take the hope *and* the clobbering, just for the change of pace.

"So?" Aliana asked. "Tell me."

Zinqued opened his mouth, but Tik'ta cut him off. "*I'll* tell you," she said firmly, "because *he* won't be honest about how crazy this whole idea is."

Crazy was good, Aliana decided. Crazy sounded just like what she wanted right now.

Damn, what had been *in* that beer? Whatever it was, another one appeared in front of her the next minute. Zinqued gave her a small nod. *My treat*, he seemed to be saying. It was Persuasion 101, but Aliana didn't mind. She lifted the mug to him, took a sip, and choked.

It was just as bad now as it had been the first time. She decided to wait for a moment before chugging it.

"You said you don't know who Barnabas is," Tik'ta said, distracting her from the taste, "so let's start there. He was something called a Ranger, apparently."

It was a good thing Aliana *hadn't* been drinking then, because if she had, she would have gotten beer up her nose. As it was, her jaw dropped open, and she gave Tik'ta an absolutely stunned look.

"A…Ranger. Like an Empress' Ranger?"

"Yes," Tik'ta said precisely. She gave Zinqued a look. "I could have told you she'd think better of it once she knew what she was getting into."

"You want to steal a ship," Aliana said, "from an Empress' Ranger." Even if she'd been a lot drunker than this, she'd have known that was a terrible plan. And then she remembered where she'd heard the name Barnabas before. "Oh, my God, and he was Ranger *One.*"

"Yes," Tik'ta said serenely, "he was."

Aliana sank her head into her hands.

She wouldn't have thought Zinqued had a hope in hell of persuading her at this point, but he was smarter than she'd given him credit for.

"If you can steal the *Shinigami*," he said quietly, "you can steal *any* ship. Having the *Shinigami* to work with would make it child's play. Whatever ship you want."

Aliana picked her head up slowly.

He swept an arm around the bar to indicate the various ship's captains. "Pick one. We won't have *any* problems taking it."

This was a bad idea. It was a bad, bad, *very* bad idea.

But she'd already made her decision. Lawrence had screwed her over eight ways to Sunday, as her Great-uncle Carter would say—she wondered what Carter was up to these days, since he'd been almost as much of a black sheep as she was—and Aliana fully intended to make her scheming husband sorry.

He'd taken her ship, her trust, and all her money, and she swore that she was going to take twice as much from him as he'd taken from her.

"Deal," she said.

CHAPTER THREE

On the lowest level of the *Shinigami* was the room that served as the gym, with mats set out for the members of the crew to spar on. Various other equipment sat unused, as Barnabas' upgrades meant he did not need to spend time honing his muscles, and the rest of the crew were various iterations of not human.

Gar had tried a few of the machines, but it had gone embarrassingly wrong in some way, and he'd somehow persuaded Shinigami not to show the videos to Barnabas. Gar had focused on sparring since then, and had recently been helping Shinigami learn how to use her new cybernetic body.

This morning, she'd decided to try sparring with Barnabas.

"I hate this," she complained. "I hate it, I hate it, I hate it, I hate it…"

"If you spent less time focusing on how much you hated

it," Barnabas said patiently, "and more time focusing on *doing* it, you'd—*oof!*"

"That'll teach you to be so superior." Shinigami, whose body could move incredibly quickly when she wanted it to, had managed to kick him halfway across the room into a wall. Now she stood with one hip jutting out and her arms crossed, a pose that would have been regal if she wasn't sticking her tongue out at him.

"So we're not going to wait for matches to start now?" Barnabas asked as he picked himself up. A rib had cracked when he hit the wall, but by the time he got to his feet it was already healed, the nanites in his blood putting it back together in a matter of seconds.

"Not if you're going to be like that," Shinigami said. She looked at Gar, laughing. "He thinks he's so—*oof!*"

"Turnabout's fair play," Barnabas warned as Shinigami went flying and hit a wall. He cracked his neck and bounced on the balls of his feet. "What were you saying? Something about me being so..."

Shinigami picked herself up with great dignity. "So *dead,*" she said, narrowing her eyes.

Barnabas gave her a grin. "Bring it on."

"I think we might want to leave," Gar said to Tafa.

"No, no," Barnabas said as Shinigami launched herself at him. "Don't leave on our account." He slid just out of the way of her attempted tackle and lashed out with one foot to catch her on her way down to the floor. "Balance, Shinigami. It's important."

"Oh, now you're just *trying* to piss me off."

"What gave it away?" Barnabas asked innocently.

"I'll tell you," Shinigami said, grabbing his leg and wrenching him over her head onto the mats, "when you're *dead*."

"Well, that seems counterproductive."

Gar and Tafa had started edging toward the door, holding themselves as close to the wall as they could. Both of them seemed determined not to make the faintest noise. When Shinigami went flying past them to hit the wall with a thud and a creak, they froze.

"Really," she said brightly, picking herself up off the floor and shaking out her joints, "you don't have to go. We wouldn't want to be rude." As Barnabas followed up his throw with a tackle, she raised her foot and planted it directly in his midsection. "Besides," she added as she threw him over one shoulder and slammed him onto the floor, "we need to discuss our next steps on the Jotun front. I had an idea, speaking of which."

"Oh?" Barnabas hooked one foot around her ankles and yanked sharply, causing her to collapse in a heap.

"Yes." By the time she was upright, he was across the room and bouncing on the balls of his feet. She gave him a glare. "A good idea, too. We're going to sneak into the Jotun Senate and get all of their data directly from there."

Barnabas stared at her, so flabbergasted that he barely made it out of the way when she came hurtling toward him again.

"That's insane," he said, as she recovered and whirled around. He ducked under her foot as she spun in a back hook kick, and then lashed out with one arm to strike her with the top of his fist. "The Jotun Senate is *extremely* well-guarded, just as well protected regarding surveillance, and... What's the other thing? Hmmm... *We don't look at all like Jotuns.*"

"Details," Shinigami said carelessly.

"You have got to be kidding me with that attitude."

"I am not, and if you'd stop punching me, I could explain."

"I thought you were the one who wanted to have this discussion while sparring," Barnabas taunted with a grin. He stopped punching, however, at which point she flipped him onto the mats and followed up with an armbar he wouldn't be able to get out of without dislocating his shoulder. "This is highly dishonorable."

"Boo hoo." Shinigami cranked on his arm slightly and grinned when he tapped out. "Where are you two going? We were going to plan, right?"

Gar and Tafa had nearly made it out the door, and now stood frozen with deer-in-the-headlights expressions.

"We were just, um..." Tafa's voice trailed off.

"We had a thing," Gar interjected.

"Yes," Tafa agreed, nodding deeply.

"Oh?" Barnabas, who had made his way to his feet again and picked an imaginary speck of dust off his arm. "What thing?"

"Well, you know, it was a...personal thing."

"Yeah," Tafa picked up again. "Personal," she added, clearly under the deeply mistaken impression that this would stop them from asking questions.

"Oh, no," Shinigami said, playing along with Barnabas. "I hope it isn't serious."

"Oh, no, no, not serious, no." Gar stared at them. "No," he added again, lamely. "Not, uh, not serious."

"Then you could probably stay to do planning with us," Shinigami suggested.

"Right?" Barnabas added, coming to stand next to her. He punched her sideways into a wall the next moment, then grinned at her. "Sorry, last one. Couldn't let you get the last hit in."

"Just you wait until we spar again," Shinigami said philosophically from the floor. "You'll break bones you didn't know you had."

"I look forward to it," Barnabas said, with a respectful nod, helping her up from the floor.

"We don't have to be there for that, do we?" Tafa sounded pained.

"I assume you'll use that time to take care of your personal thing," Barnabas said innocently.

Both of them stared at him for a moment.

"Right," Gar said finally. His double-pupiled eyes narrowed slightly as he tried to decide if Barnabas was mocking him.

Barnabas saw no reason to clear things up. "So, Shinigami...how were you thinking we'd get into the Senate buildings?"

Shinigami sat up and started diagnostics on one of her forearms. She was so realistic-looking that it was a bit jarring to see her pop a patch of unremarkable skin open and begin fiddling with display panels and metal struts.

"Fake suits," she said, as she worked. She looked up with a grin. "Jotuns wear suits, so can we."

"We have stuff in our midsections that *isn't* a tank with a Jotun in it, though."

"Yeah, I was working on that part," she said contemplatively.

"So you don't *actually* have a plan."

"I said I had an *idea*. But...no, I do not have a plan."

"I wondered." Barnabas leaned against the wall and thought. "My first instinct is that it's too risky by far. What's the benefit of doing it this way?"

"Thought you might ask that," Shinigami said with satisfaction. "The benefit is that we get to it before Jeltor thinks to, and then *he* doesn't have that on his record."

"Ahhh." Barnabas understood now. "Why didn't you lead with that?" All of them had been worried about Jeltor since he'd been accused of treason. Although the charges were in the process of being cleared—Barnabas having essentially blackmailed the entire Senate—it would hardly look good for Jeltor to have more on his record.

Especially since he had been with them a week ago when they killed a senator. That hadn't been the plan, it was just the way things had shaken out. On the other hand, "it was just the way things shook out" wasn't a stellar legal defense.

So it made good sense to keep him out of this operation.

Barnabas tapped his fingers on his arm as he thought. Not only was he human, which was noteworthy enough in this sector, but he was also, well, *him*. He wouldn't be surprised if the Jotuns had alarms keyed to his biosignature somehow.

"Send me," Tafa said suddenly.

Everyone's head swiveled, and for a moment no one could think of anything to say.

"I'm sorry?" Barnabas said at last, politely.

Tafa rolled her eyes. "Yofu are often mechanics. I can pretend to be a mechanic and carry a case that includes part of Shinigami—a communications hub that would allow her to tap into their systems remotely. And I don't think the Jotun know who I am, unlike you and possibly Gar."

"They don't know who I am, either," Shinigami pointed out.

"They might," Tafa argued. "Who knows if anyone was watching the fight between you and Biset? They *might* recognize you—and, again, Yofu are often mechanics. It wouldn't be out of the question for a Yofu to be fixing something in a random hallway. It would for a human."

The rest of the group looked at one another warily. Tafa was an established member of the crew now, someone who could make any of them smile on a bad day, whose paintings now hung in many hallways, and who had assisted in the non-combat parts of a few missions. But she *hadn't* ever been involved in something that could turn into combat, and all of them were worried about what might happen if things went south.

Barnabas, however, was not going to take her offer lightly. Tafa had grown up under the constant threat of violence, and if she were willing to go into danger, he wouldn't insult her by rejecting her offer out of hand.

Instead, he looked at her gravely. "It would be very

helpful. As you say, you wouldn't attract the suspicion we would. We just need to come up with a backup plan so that if they find out what you're doing, we can get you out of there safely."

Tafa gave him a grateful smile as she nodded. She had clearly been afraid that he would simply reject her offer, and with Barnabas taking her seriously, her happiness was plain to see.

"I bet Shinigami could learn some of the camera patterns and put in false feeds," she suggested. "That way, you could be close in case something went wrong."

"And I can also have alerts set up in their system so we'll have warning if they send guards or engage defensive systems," Shinigami pointed out. "They won't have an easy time taking us by surprise."

"You should take a breathing mask in your mechanic's bag," Gar added. "That way, if they try to fill the place with water, you can get out fine."

"Do we have breathing masks that can fit her?" Barnabas asked Shinigami.

"No, but we can find one between here and there," she replied. She finished her diagnostics and closed the panel on her arm so that it once more looked like unbroken skin. "And figure out the cameras, and figure out where we might be able to plug into their system. The sort of information we're looking for will be on an unconnected server —if they're smart, that is, which I've started to think they might be."

"Unfortunate," Barnabas said drily.

She shot him a smile as she got to her feet. "Very. On

the other hand, as you're fond of saying, it's good to have worthy enemies."

"So we're doing this?" Gar asked, half in disbelief.

"I think so." Barnabas nodded to Tafa. "She made a good suggestion."

"And I can't let you guys have *all* the fun," Tafa said with a grin.

CHAPTER FOUR

"Excellency." One of Grisor's aides appeared in the doorway. "We have landed."

Grisor's personal tank was being lowered into his suit. He had spent the journey relaxing in a water-filled compartment within his ship, hunting fish and thinking about what he was about to see.

It had been a contemplative journey. Grisor did not take this event lightly. What was happening today—hopefully, he would arrive in time to see it—was the culmination of many years' worth of research and planning.

The idea for the Infrastructure Revitalization Committee had not come from Grisor, but instead from his mentor, a senator whose utter hatred of other species had at first seemed ridiculous. The younger Jotun had believed in his species' superiority, of course, as any reasonable Jotun would, but he had found his mentor's vitriol to be indelicate and unnecessary.

At first.

Then Grisor had seen the way other species conducted themselves. The Brakalons were always eager for a fight, and the Shrillexians were even worse, selling themselves as mercenaries for the thrill of violence. The Yofu were respectable enough but had no ambition. The Hieto and Ubuara had similarly made nothing of themselves. The list went on. One species inspired respect, and that was the Kurtherians—but even they were divided against themselves, and that weakness might prove fatal.

Grisor's mentor had died without ever receiving his due from the Senate. His ideas were laughed at, and at the end of his life, he lost the support of his province and was replaced by someone younger and more in favor of open trade and diplomacy. Anger simmered in Grisor as he watched these events play out.

His mentor had dreamed of a sector ruled by the Jotuns, and Grisor had seen that his own people would be the first stumbling block. Too many of them were short-sighted, secure enough in the idea of their superiority that they did not wish to cement it in any way. They used it as an excuse for laziness, just as Grisor once had.

He had thought long and hard about this. Many of his colleagues believed that the greatest good they could do in the Senate was to represent the will of the people. Grisor did not. He believed that the greatest good he could do was the right thing for his people, whether or not they believed they wanted it.

And he didn't intend to give them the chance to think about it.

Now settled into the biosuit, he strode out of his chambers and through the spaceship, his aide behind him. At the doors that led to the gangway, four soldiers waited for him. There were dangerous aliens in this facility, and Grisor did not take unnecessary risks.

Just look what had happened to Biset, after all.

At the door to the facility, he was met by two Jotuns who looked so alike that he blinked. Both of them took a single knee, a sign of deep respect. The gesture had been adopted from other species, as it was generally difficult to accomplish in a biosuit.

Grisor felt a wave of satisfaction. The researchers here were at the forefront of his plan, and it did his heart good to see them show such reverence. Soon, every Jotun would do so, of course, and every Brakalon and Torcellan and every other sentient alien in this sector—and beyond.

But he would remember these as some of the first to do so.

"We are honored by your visit," said one of them as he stood.

"We have made every effort in pursuit of your goals," said the second. "We think you will be pleased by our progress, and hope you will tour the entire facility during your visit if time permits."

Grisor gave a ripple of regret. "Nothing would give me more pleasure. However, I have little time." In fact, he should not really be here at all, but how could he miss this of all days? "I have come to see the first step toward our new world."

The two researchers looked at one another nervously, and Grisor had the vague thought that they hadn't looked this much alike the last time he had seen them. Perhaps people who worked together in remote facilities for years at a time began to resemble one another.

He was more concerned with that look, however. "What is it?"

"The process is proceeding," the first hastened to say.

"But slowly," said the second.

"Does this mean," Grisor said, hiding his impatience, "that I will *not* see a conversion today?"

Both researchers took a knee once more.

"We have failed you," one of them said.

"He is much stronger than we anticipated," added the other. "We do not doubt that he will turn in time, but the progress is much slower than in our previous converts."

Grisor considered this, saying nothing. Although he was disappointed with the situation, he was not angry with the researchers. It made sense, in a way, that a Naval captain would be resistant to the training. Captains only made it into the Naval Academy when they had extraordinary self-control and mental discipline. He should have expected that this conversion would take longer than the others.

He did not say any of this, however. It did not do any harm to have the researchers be upset about failing him.

"Show me," he said finally.

They exchanged a worried glance but stood and led him into the facility without hesitation. Moaning and shrieking came from the floors above them, along with some heavy crashes.

"What is that sound?" Grisor asked in distaste.

"Early iterations of our experiments were not so successful," one of the researchers explained.

"We find the failed experiments to be useful, however," said the other, perhaps anticipating Grisor's question of, "Why didn't you just kill them?"

"We wish to know if rehabilitation is possible," said the first, or possibly the second. Grisor was still having trouble determining which had spoken. The same one continued, "Perhaps in other species, as in the Jotuns, there are variations. Every success and failure will be useful later."

They were conscientious and had thought of complications he might not anticipate. Grisor liked that.

Then they emerged into the research chamber, and every other thought went out of his head.

In a tank at the center of the room was Captain Jeltor, writhing in pain as chemicals worked their way into his body and words and images were imprinted on his mind. Grisor recognized him at once. His photo had been everywhere during the incident with the Yennai Corporation and the ensuing trial for treason.

Unlike many in the Senate, Grisor had no especial distaste for Jeltor. In fact, he understood some of the male's motivations. Many in the Senate would have been perfectly content to have the Yennai Corporation run the Jotun government.

Clearly, this was unacceptable. Grisor would never have allowed it—and, with the technology to turn any mind to his purpose, there would have been no danger of such a thing happening.

Jeltor had not known that, and thus his struggle against the Yennai Corporation was understandable and forgivable. Had he stopped there, perhaps, Grisor might even have approached him as an equal and made him an offer.

But Jeltor persisted in following the lead of the human, Barnabas. Like Barnabas, he showed a remarkable drive toward individualistic thought. And Jeltor had been there when Biset was killed, even hearing the name of the Committee from the mysterious assassin—who Grisor had so far been unable to trace.

Jeltor was unlikely to embrace Grisor's vision, so he would be converted. The process would leave his mental faculties intact—earlier experiments had not been so successful at this—but Jeltor would obey any order given to him by a member of the Committee, and would be loyal to Grisor above all.

It would be a peaceful existence. In Grisor's opinion, there was a great deal of unnecessary despair in the world, born of divided loyalties and uncertainty. He would eliminate that.

It was just a pity that the process was so much more painful than the outcome.

Grisor walked in a long, slow circle around the tank. He could not quite hear the words that were being said, but he knew what they were. He had been one of the ones to create the tapes, after all, and he had chosen the sentiments with great care.

Jeltor was being bombarded with images and words ordering him to give his obedience to Grisor and the Committee while the chemicals that flooded his tank were lowering his mental barriers.

"What mix of chemicals did you end up choosing?" Grisor asked the two researchers curiously.

"There are many mixes," one of them said.

"Depending on the part of the process," said the other.

"And the individual," finished the second.

"And you say he's making progress?" Grisor asked idly. "How can you tell?" He was curious, no more.

"It is…complex," said one of them. "The way they fight, the chemicals their bodies produce. Such things, we have seen in other species during the process."

"And you're sure that he will convert, not simply break?" Jeltor was the perfect tool to infiltrate any unruly resistance. Losing him would be a blow.

Now they paused. "One can never be entirely sure," one of them said finally. His voice trembled slightly on the words. "We have made the process as streamlined as possible. Losses have been rare, and there have been none recently. But it *is* possible."

"Thank you for your honesty." Grisor would remember this. Many who aspired to power made the mistake of punishing subordinates for giving them honest answers. Grisor found this to be unforgivably stupid. The practice only encouraged subordinates to lie.

He watched Jeltor for another long moment. It was disappointing, Grisor thought, that he would not be able to see Jeltor's conversion today.

He could wait. He nodded to the researchers. "Contact me when he has been converted. I will need to speak with him immediately. To the guards, he added, "You will remain here. Give the researchers any assistance they require. Protect them from the experiments, if need be, or anyone who should try to find and destroy this facility."

He swept from the room without another word and was back on his ship within minutes.

He only had to wait a little longer, and he would have everything he had been working for.

Left behind in the laboratory, Gil and Wev stared at the tank and used their silent communications interface to speak to one another.

We must turn off the machines, Gil said. *We cannot risk this captain being turned to the Committee's purposes.*

Wait, for now, Wev argued. *The guards are still watching. We must take care not to make them think we are hiding anything.*

Both of them stole a glance at the side of the room, where a closet hid what remained of the real research team. Gil and Wev, agents with the Jotun Interplanetary Intelligence Agency, had been sent to investigate the Committee's activity—and disrupt it.

Disrupt it, they had. They were still untangling the various threads of it. However, they were alone in this operation, not daring to call for help lest they tip someone off to the fact that Intelligence was beginning to move against the members of the Committee. They still did not even know who all those members *were.*

They had identified Huword first, and then Biset. Now they knew of a third: Grisor.

But now they found themselves in a tricky situation. What would the guards be monitoring? How carefully must Gil and Wev pretend to follow the research proce-dures—or must they truly continue the work that had been started here?

In unison, they looked at the tank that held Jeltor. With silent sharing of thoughts, and so many years spent working together, they had become more alike than they were different.

Neither of them liked torture, but both of them would do it—if it meant destroying the Committee before the Committee destroyed the Jotuns.

CHAPTER FIVE

Hevarod was not quite as Barnabas remembered it. The last time he had been here, the skies had been clear and the weather warm, and waves had lapped gently at the shore with a soothing sound.

It was winter now.

The sky was an iron gray that was matched only by the deep white-capped swells of the water, and the waves pounded against the sea walls remorselessly. The walls kept out the water...mostly. While the pathways and streets of the aboveground portion of the city were not *flooded*, they were certainly wet.

"How did the Jotuns survive here?" Barnabas asked incredulously. He was picturing the Jotuns outside their mechanical suits, but in their natural form as large jellyfish, and even from inside the *Shinigami's* shuttle, he could sense the coldness of the water and the heavy churn of the waves. Surely a Jotun outside its suit would be crushed.

Shinigami, however, gave him a bemused smile. "How

did humans survive in all those places on Earth? Species adapt and develop rudimentary technology. The Jotuns probably began in a more even climate, as humans did on Earth—and then spread."

Barnabas nodded. She had a good point. When he thought of some of the places he'd seen on Earth, from the Alps and the Himalayas to the desolate landscapes of Alaska and Montana to the wastes of the great, shifting deserts, he realized that human survival was no less precarious.

When TOM had crashed on Earth, he reflected, the Kurtherian had been lucky there had been any humans to join with.

The *Shinigami* itself remained in orbit around Jotuna, cloaked and learning all it could of the Jotun satellites and their programming. Shinigami knew enough about their systems to keep the ship and its shuttle hidden—as far as they could tell—but the finer points of Jotun computer systems were still, as she put it, "hidden behind programming like a blob of grape jelly."

Barnabas, whose idea of a good night was a paper book, and who still wrote on paper with a fountain pen, had no idea what she meant by that. He accepted that it was her forte, and trusted that she would tell him if she really needed help.

He suspected that she was just grumbling. Shinigami had not yet come across any system she could not quickly learn and work against.

Instead of attracting attention by landing outside the city, the team had decided to land in the main set of docks. Shinigami had changed the electronic signature of the shuttle, and as far as they knew, the Jotuns would not know it by sight—certainly not well enough to program their surveillance cameras to pick it up.

They were pretending to be Yofu, so it was Tafa who had guided the shuttle down, answering questions from air traffic control in her Yofu accent. She was dressed in blue coveralls that had a respectable number of grease stains on them. She had gotten them on a nearby station, where she'd had trouble convincing a bemused mechanic that she actually *wanted* the dirty uniform and would buy him a new and clean one. He had clearly thought she was crazy, but money was money, and she now had a uniform that looked well-worn, with a name stitched on the chest: *Kila*.

Once they had sat through the interminable landing pattern and finally gotten a bay, she vacated the pilot's chair and began assembling her tools. A big mechanic's bag, looking far too heavy for her small frame, was loaded with screwdrivers, welding tools, and some things Barnabas assumed were wrenches.

"You're sure you don't need to be closer?" she asked Shinigami anxiously.

"Quite sure," Shinigami said, giving Barnabas a wink over Tafa's head. She had tried to explain that her actual processing took place on the ship and that the location of her body really didn't matter at all, but Tafa didn't seem to believe it.

Barnabas crouched to examine the handles of the bag. The Yofu had double-thumbed hands, and so everything from their tools to the fastenings on their clothes was constructed slightly differently.

"How are you feeling?" he asked Tafa carefully. He

41

didn't look at her, and he kept his voice casual. He didn't want to make her anxious.

She wasn't fooled. She gave him a glare. "You mean, do I want to call it off? No. I don't."

"Just checking," Barnabas said. *And your implant is working well?* he added silently.

Yes, just like it was on the ship. She gave him another glare and then sighed. "I'm sorry. I don't mean to be rude, I'm just..." She swallowed.

"It's normal to be nervous before a mission," Barnabas told her gently. "For anyone, even when it's not their first mission."

"*You* don't get nervous," she said quietly.

"Not often—but I sometimes do. Gar can verify that."

"He's a robot," Gar said amusedly. "He's never been nervous in his life. But I get nervous all the time."

Barnabas laughed. He wasn't immune to worry, as others seemed to think he was. He had simply learned over the years to let his worry exist without overwhelming him, and he was careful to manage it through meditation and action rather than dwelling on it. Decades as a monk would do that to a person.

He suspected that Gar was much the same. The Luvendi were apparently very fond of meditating, viewing it as a cornerstone of their society. Even though Gar had left his home planet and did not think much of its limitations, he likely had the skills to control his worry before a mission.

"Besides," said Shinigami, "say the Jotun police come up to you and say, 'Hey, what are you doing here?' We have a plan. You'll say..." She raised her eyebrow and gestured for Tafa to go on.

Tafa had quite a flair for the dramatic, which they had discovered while planning the mission. She fluttered her hands slightly and widened her eyes. "I'm here for the repairs to the main circuits," she said, sounding appropriately nervous. She dug around in her pockets, making a great show of looking for documentation, and pulled out several folded pieces of paper, which fluttered to the floor around her in a carefully-contrived and accidental-looking bit of clumsiness.

"Oh, I'm so sorry. I know it's here somewhere. Here's my permit, here's my landing clearance. I know I have my landing bay receipt somewhere. Just one moment—I'm *so* sorry—and here's my licensing paperwork." She handed it to Shinigami, her face shining with honesty. "As you can see, I've served many apprentice hours, and I've worked on Jotun circuitry before. There won't be any problems. I think Mr...." she "checked" her other paperwork, "Hilar will be very pleased with my work. You've subcontracted the very best." She said the last words with the practiced smile of someone giving a sales pitch.

Barnabas and Gar were looking on with amusement while Shinigami puffed herself up and pretended to be part of the Jotun Senate's police force.

"Miss, this permit is for a house. *This* is the *Senate.*"

Tafa widened her eyes even more. "No! No, it can't be, because I followed the instructions very carefully. Ferdy wrote them down for me, see? Once you come out the east entrance of the docks, you turn left, and then you go three blocks, and then you turn *right*—oh, no. Oh, no, I turned left!" She sounded miserable. She grabbed for the papers, and Barnabas only just caught the quick motion of her hand that flung a bot onto the ground behind Shinigami. "I'm so sorry, I'm *so* sorry. Do you know the way to Manrel Hilar's house?"

"Good!" Shinigami said enthusiastically. She knelt and retrieved the tiny bot, who had been trying determinedly to find an entry point into the walls of the shuttle. "Come here, you. You'll get to climb around all you want later."

"It's not sentient, you know," Barnabas told her. "It worries me that you talk to them."

She grinned at him. "Do you think I'm gathering my troops for a robot uprising?"

"I don't know! I wouldn't put it past you."

"You're wise not to," she replied blandly. After this somewhat worrisome sentiment, she told Tafa, "And see? You'll be fine. You're a born actress."

Tafa glowed with pleasure. She had retrieved the little bot and put it in her cuff pocket, and was now lifting a small processing core into the bag. The core had a remote wipe and self-destruct, which were contained nicely so that the core would not explode, and had multiple tools to attach to different pieces of the system. Tafa and Shinigami would work together to find offices with hidden data banks and would do all they could to get the data extracted and analyzed before they were noticed.

They were starting with Biset's offices, which would not yet be closed off since his death had not been announced. Hopefully, searching his systems for mentions of the Infrastructure Revitalization Committee would provide a trail of clues they could follow.

Meanwhile, Shinigami and Gar would take one route to approach the Senate buildings, and Barnabas would take another. If Tafa got into trouble, they would be able to get her out quickly. Shinigami could even remotely pilot the shuttle to their location if necessary.

Barnabas was hoping it wouldn't come to that, but he was glad to have a contingency plan.

Tafa finished packing the bag and stood. She hoisted it onto her shoulders like a backpack and nodded at the group.

"I'm going to go," she told them. There was determination in her tone—but also excitement. "Meet back here in a couple of hours?"

"Sounds good." Barnabas gave her a grin and a handshake.

They watched as she set off, a small figure making her way determinedly through the chaos of the docks. She had her part down well, even stopping a passing Yofu to ask him directions to Manrel Hilar's house. The house was real, after all, as was the construction project, and Hilar was a notable figure in Hevarod. Her story would attract no suspicion.

"We're good to go," Barnabas said to Gar and Shinigami. "Let's get into position. You two go first, so if they stop me, they'll have less chance of getting you, too."

"Good call." Gar did a last check of his weapons and armor. "Ready?" he asked Shinigami.

"Ready." She adjusted her own armor, all of it slim-fitting and easily mistaken for normal street clothes, and put her purse over one shoulder. Since they didn't want to attract attention to the veritable arsenal she carried, she had put her guns in the purse. It made Barnabas laugh every time he saw it.

They walked away as he watched, and he gave a small smile.

Jeltor was going to be amused when they told him about this.

CHAPTER SIX

Aliana made her way through the crush of Border Station 7 toward the docks that generally held less affluent merchants—in most cases, smugglers. She liked this area a lot more than the docks higher up, each with a nice, shiny ship in it, and each ship with its slimy captain.

If she were honest, she was worried she'd see her own ship there.

And Lawrence.

She ducked her head to blink away the tears in her eyes and collided with a man with blue eyes and short blond hair. Aliana was pretty tall, so she was looking slightly down, but from the amount of muscle he had, she knew at once that she had no desire to ever get in a fight with him.

So, out of sheer survival instinct, therefore, she fell all over herself to apologize: "I am *so* sorry, I didn't mean to bump into you. I wasn't looking where I was going and—"

"Hey, whoa." He gave a little laugh and rubbed his head,

where a white scar showed near his hairline. "It was an accident. I'm not worried about it."

"Oh." She frowned at him suspiciously, but he certainly didn't *seem* angry.

"*You* okay?" he asked. He peered at her, and she had the uncomfortable sense that he saw the tears.

"Yeah." She hiked her bag up on her shoulder. "I'm fine. All fine." He was still looking at her, seeing a lot more than she wanted him to see, so she cleared her throat decisively. "I have to go."

"Hey." He caught her arm as she ducked around him. It was a light touch, not meant to be intimidating, but she could tell how strong he was. And he had good reflexes, because she'd tried to keep her arm out of his reach. "Look, it's not a big deal or anything, but if you're in trouble—not now, I guess, but whenever—you can always look me up. I'm Magistrate... Never mind that. I'm Buster. Or 'Busta-move,' if you like nicknames." His smile didn't falter even under her flat stare. "Take care of yourself," he said and disappeared into the crowd with her staring after him.

Aliana blinked, then shook herself. He seemed nice, but no one was just *nice* in this world—or, if they were, they were going to get taken advantage of and wind up dead in a ditch somewhere. Either way, she didn't want anything to do with this guy.

She was still shaking her head as she approached the docking bay Zinqued had specified, 486A, and got her first look at the ship.

It wasn't bad, as ships went. Something was painted on the side in flowing alien letters, with PALPARI printed beneath. She wondered if the two things even sounded vaguely the same. From what she'd heard of the Hieto language, it was filled with hisses and pops that a human mouth couldn't precisely reproduce.

"Aliana." Zinqued had appeared at the top of the gangway. "Glad to see you. Tik'ta kept telling me that you'd think better of it and not show up, but I told her you would."

Aliana gave him a smile despite herself. She liked the way Tik'ta looked after her captain despite her obvious exasperation, and something about the two of them made her feel like this would be a nice, safe job.

Well, a job that wouldn't make her run into Lawrence, anyway—and that was all she really cared about. From a few murmured words they'd exchanged, she guessed that they generally operated in a whole different sector, which was exactly the sort of thing Aliana was looking for in a job.

"Why did you think I'd come back if Tik'ta didn't?" she asked Zinqued. *Her new captain,* she reminded herself. She shouldn't call him by his name. Some aliens were *really* offended by poor etiquette.

"I know the look," Zinqued said. He stepped back to let her into the ship. "It's the same across all species."

"What look?"

"Hunger." Zinqued looked at her. "It doesn't matter what it's for. For some people it's money, for others it's a mate or power. You're hungry for something, and this job can help you get it."

Aliana said nothing for a moment. She was chewing over the thought in her head. *Hungry.* Was she hungry?

Yes. She had been screwed over, and she'd accepted

defeat without even questioning it...until Zinqued came along and showed her that she had another choice. That she could get back what was hers and maybe have some revenge in the bargain.

Who was she kidding? The revenge was the main draw now. She wanted Lawrence to suffer. She wanted him to lose everything, and spend his days as broken down as she had been. She smiled at Zinqued.

"Yeah," she agreed, "this job can get me what I want."

"And what's that?" he asked.

He seemed more curious than anything else, not exactly *ordering* her to tell him, so Aliana just smiled and gave a little shrug. "My business for now. I'll tell you when we've stolen the *Shinigami* and you're helping me steal the second ship."

"Ah." He seemed almost pleased by the way she played her cards close to the chest. "I will look forward to it, then. And you won't be disappointed—we've been doing this for a long time. We know our way around these things."

He had shown Aliana through several low passages as they spoke, and now he gestured to a small cabin. "This is yours."

"I have it to myself?" Aliana was pleasantly surprised. She was alone on her bucket of bolts, but on every other ship she'd lived on, she'd shared her living quarters. Sometimes it hadn't been so bad, of course. She hadn't minded sharing that little cabin with—

James. Her throat seemed to close, and she blinked back tears all of a sudden. She'd been a mess since all of this had kicked off, it seemed like. Two weeks ago, she'd been content to spend her evenings getting drunk and starting bar fights, which to her ranked above crying alone in a tiny ship's cabin.

To distract herself, she asked Zinqued, "So what's different about this ship?"

He had been turning to leave, but he looked back at her with interest. He cocked his head to the side, not quite sure what she meant.

"Not…" Aliana pointed at the floor. "The *Palpari*?"

He seemed to find this very funny. "Close enough." He pronounced it in Hieto and she picked out some similar sounds, but knew she'd never be able to pull it off.

"Right. Not this ship, the one you're trying to steal? You said you've tried before." Aliana dumped her bag out on the bed and began pulling drawers open and putting shirts and coveralls inside. "Never met a ship thief who had it bad for a specific ship. Kind of thought you guys were opportunists."

"I was." Zinqued sounded almost grumpy. "You have to see this ship to understand it," he added, and she realized he wasn't grumpy about being called a thief or an opportunist. He was grumpy about having the weakness of wanting a specific ship.

She fought the urge to laugh.

"It's a beautiful ship," he continued, and his gaze was distant. He leaned in the doorway, almost a human gesture. "The lines, the way it moves, its weapons…"

"You know they aren't going to give you more Federation missiles," Aliana pointed out.

"The ability to shoot them is enough. People are always coming up with new things. With that ship, I can get whatever I need." He was completely confident. "And with you on board, we'll be able to get it. You knew about the Rangers. You can figure out the ship's weaknesses."

A normal person, Aliana thought, would admit they didn't know much about Rangers and didn't think the ships *had* weaknesses.

She'd never been one to let trivial things like facts stand in the way of her goals, though. She'd done a lot of things she had been told she couldn't do, after all, and she wasn't about to go back to being a scared little kid who let other people tell her what was and wasn't possible.

So she nodded. "Yeah," she said, and she meant it. She wasn't bullshitting him. She was promising that no matter how impossible it seemed, she'd get the job done.

Right now, she was wondering why it seemed so simple to believe it when it came to someone else's goals but not her own.

She'd think about that later. She nodded to him and he left, clearly pleased. She kept unpacking, humming to herself. This ship wasn't bad. A lot of people complained about ships, but Aliana liked them. There wasn't too much space, everything had its purpose, and it kept her from getting complacent—waking up to the same thing day in and day out.

She was still humming when there was a rap on the door. She looked around to see Tik'ta there.

"Hey," Aliana said. She was a bit wary. She knew that Tik'ta wasn't exactly glad that Aliana had signed on.

"Hello," Tik'ta said. She looked around the small room. "May I come in?"

Fitting two people in here was going to be awkward,

but Aliana wanted to be polite—and she was curious. She stepped back a little. "Sure."

Tik'ta came in and closed the door behind her. She seemed a bit nervous, and she clasped her hands and swayed a little before speaking. "I have been looking up the culture of your people so that I can explain the captain's interest in the *Shinigami*."

Aliana frowned and leaned against the back wall, bracing her foot and crossing her arms. She wasn't aware that this was really a cultural thing—Zinqued certainly hadn't mentioned it.

"I believe the proper way to describe this," Tik'ta said, still awkwardly formal, "is that the *Shinigami* is the captain's 'white whale.'" She paused, seemingly to be waiting for something.

The phrase meant nothing to Aliana. "What's a white whale?" she said finally. "Other than, you know...a white whale." She scratched her head.

"It is a reference to something that is pursued obsessively," Tik'ta explained. She sounded agitated now, as if she had hoped that Aliana would have had a different reaction. "I was given to understand that humans would understand this reference. It is in your dictionaries. A librarian at the archives told me—"

"I'm gonna stop you right there. Librarians are not exactly..." Aliana considered, "normal," she finished. "They like to think that everyone should know everything." She snorted in derision. "Me, I think if you've got something to say, you should just say it straight out, not try to talk about — What *is* a white whale, though?"

"It is a reference to a book."

"Right. If you want to say something, just *say* it. Don't bother with old references. Is that from Earth or something?"

"I don't know." Tik'ta sounded a bit lost. "I only wanted you to understand."

"Right." Aliana rubbed her face. "I... Thank you, that was considerate." Tik'ta hadn't *meant* to make her want to bang her head against the wall, after all. "You say it's an obsession?"

"I think, like Ahab—that's the captain in the book—he will pursue it to his death." Tik'ta seemed worried. "I do not blame you for signing on. I'm sure you have your reasons, and he would only find someone else if it weren't you. But this may be dangerous, so you should know what you're getting into. I don't think you'll ever get to collect on your bargain," she said honestly.

Aliana thought about this. Tik'ta was trying to be nice again; she could tell.

"Why do *you* stay, then?" she asked. She narrowed her eyes. "You're not a slave, are you?"

"No!" Tik'ta seemed to find this quite funny. "No, I'm not. I could leave if I wanted to." She shook her head. "I don't know why I stay. To look after him, I guess. I've had captains who were idiots, and captains who were cruel. He's a lunatic, but he's not mean." She gave a gesture that Aliana guessed was a shrug.

"I'll stay, then," Aliana said.

Tik'ta stared at her.

"Look, you're clearly trying to warn me off for my own good, but you don't have anywhere to go and neither do I."

Aliana started unpacking again. "By the way, I don't *ever* want to talk about that."

Tik'ta hesitated, then nodded again. "Then I welcome you aboard. We will have food soon, in the galley."

She left, and Aliana looked after her for a moment before shrugging. As long as she got paid, she told herself, she didn't care whether or not this job was going to be successful. If Zinqued didn't figure out how to steal her ship back for her, she'd find a way to do it herself.

In the meantime, she'd be gone from Federation space and unlikely to run into Lawrence.

She'd take that deal.

CHAPTER SEVEN

Tafa walked quickly through the district surrounding the Jotun government buildings. Hevarod was a pleasant enough city, or at least it probably was when the weather wasn't cold and stormy. Perhaps because the sea was so violent today, the entire place seemed to be filled with people.

She figured this was good. More people meant less of a chance that she'd stand out, and she'd learned long ago that one should never stand out. The problem with being the daughter of the family "traitors," as she had been, was that you were always being watched. You were always noteworthy.

Tafa's parents had been part of a family that produced weapons and had worked toward peace—against the family interests. When she was young, they were taken away. The family held them in a prison far away and had them tortured for years until they finally died.

Tafa had always known that the same could happen to

her. Over the years, she had grieved her parents and sometimes resented them for their principles. After all, those principles had resulted in them being taken away, and in her living under the shadow of suspicion. She had begun to make her peace with it, but she felt like she'd spent her whole life learning to be boring and forgettable, and she'd gotten so good at it that her own relatives had failed to pay attention to her most of the time.

If she could be boring enough for them not to notice her, she could certainly be boring enough for people in a crowd not to notice her. Tafa threaded her way through the people, making sure to keep her face up and her body relaxed. If you looked down, you looked like you had something to hide; like you were *trying* not to be noticed.

So she kept a smile on her face and made sure to take out her directions every now and then to study them whenever she saw a police officer glancing her way. That way, some of the police might say later that they *had* seen her, and it would give credence to her tale of being lost.

She told herself that she knew how to do this, but her heart was still beating fast as she made her way down a side street and into the alleys around the Senate building. The closer she got, the more instinctive it was to hunch her shoulders and do other things that people would find noteworthy, and she couldn't afford to do that.

Almost there, Shinigami said in her mind. *How are you feeling?*

I wish everyone would stop asking that, Tafa snapped crossly. *It just makes me more nervous.* Too late, she realized she'd spoken to everyone, not just Shinigami. *Sorry.*

Not to worry, Barnabas replied, sounding unperturbed.

Yeah, Gar added. *Takes a few tries to get it right. I think I mind-shouted my first few conversations at Barnabas.*

From Barnabas' internal laughter this was an accurate statement, and Tafa struggled not to laugh along with them. With her uniform and work bag, she wasn't very noteworthy here, but if she burst out laughing at a conversation no one else could hear, she certainly would be.

She joined the stream of people going in through the maintenance entrances. Most were Jotuns, and a few gave her a second glance—but no more than that. It had been a worthwhile investment to get an old jumpsuit because no one questioned her when she had years' worth of grease stains on her clothes. Tafa curled her hands tight around the straps of the backpack, so that no one would see her relatively pristine fingernails, and allowed herself to be carried along a lower corridor with the bulk of the workers.

She didn't need to go anywhere in particular at this point. Shinigami was using the scanners in the cube to assess the structure, and there was no way for Tafa to know yet which direction she needed to go. She tried to look purposeful, and still a little weary—as if she were tired of this job as an electrical engineer.

"Hey," a voice said in the tone of a police officer trying to stop someone.

Tafa's heart leapt into her throat, but she kept walking. There was no reason to think they were talking to her, and the worst thing she could do would be to look guilty.

"Hey, you," the voice said again. There was a clank, and the crowd began to swirl around her. "You, Yofu—with the backpack."

Tafa stopped, her heart pounding and her mouth suddenly dry. She turned to look at the police officer.

"I'm sorry," she said automatically.

Stay calm, Barnabas advised her. *Keep your wits about you. You can do this, Tafa.*

With renewed confidence, Tafa smiled up at the Senate police officer and dug in her pockets. "Do you need to see my permit?"

"Where are you going?" the officer asked suspiciously.

"Oh! I…" Tafa pulled out one of the pieces of paper and studied it. "I don't know, actually," she said, after a few moments. "My boss said to meet him here. He needed the other set of tools." She hunched her shoulders and hoisted the backpack to indicate it. "He said if I went in the back door and just followed where people were going… Well, look, I don't know if you've seen him. He's Yofu, and he has a high nose bridge, and his eyes are a little bit canted forward—"

"I don't know who you're talking about," the police officer interrupted her. He was bobbing in his tank impatiently. "Just figure out where you're going. You can't just wander around government buildings with no clearance. You'll need to go down that way to get your tools scanned."

"Oh! Right. Thanks." Tafa smiled up at him and started off in the direction he was pointing. "Sorry again," she added over her shoulder.

He just grunted. He was already looking at the rest of the workers coming into the building, all in their chef's uniforms or cleaning gear.

Keep walking a bit more, Shinigami said when Tafa slowed. *You're close to a lift. Keep going. Now take out your permit and pretend to look at it. Give it a moment—I'm putting the security cameras on a loop. Now look to see if he's watching you.*

He's not.

Up the lift when it opens. Do it quickly.

Tafa pushed her way into the lift, heart pounding. She half-expected alarms to sound, but nothing happened. The Jotun who had come out of the lift when it stopped thudded away without giving her a second glance.

Now what?

Give me a moment while I get the lift moving. A second later, it shuddered into motion. *Good,* Shinigami said. *They don't guard the exits off that hallway very well, but they require a pretty complicated verification to get the lifts moving so no one can use them by accident. I'm taking you to the fourth floor. That's where I'm guessing the system I scanned is.*

The lift stopped, and Tafa made sure she was studying her piece of paper as the door opened. She walked out slowly and pretended to finish reading before setting off to the right as Shinigami instructed.

With the directions being muttered in her ear, she soon arrived at a doorway flanked by two guards.

The committee was guarding Biset's rooms. Tafa's heart began to pound again, but she remembered Barnabas' reassurance. She could do this. She pointed at the door tentatively.

"I was supposed to lock some of the electrical systems down in here?" she asked as if their presence made her unsure of the directive. Then she strengthened her voice, sliding into the language she'd practiced with Shinigami—using facts and terminology to make their eyes glaze over and give them the idea that she knew what she was talking about. Shinigami had told her that in a lie, too many specifics were better than too few. "They wanted to make sure they were on different circuits and not available from the main systems," Tafa explained to the guards. "I'll need to access panel circuits 2 and…" She checked her paperwork. "And 7," she finished. "Then the senator won't have to worry about *anyone* getting into his data."

The guards were here to make sure no one went into Biset's rooms, but they hadn't been told why, and Tafa's mission sounded like the sort of thing their employers would want. They nodded and opened the door for her, and she left it open on purpose as she settled down to work. When one of them reached out to shut it, leaving her alone, she gave him a distracted smile but otherwise pretended not to notice.

There were security cameras in two corners of the room, so Tafa made sure to have her back to them as she knelt and swung the bag off her back. She let the bots out when her hand was hidden from the cameras and set about laying out her tools.

She knew enough about electrical work to pretend to do the work she'd said she was doing, and she made sure to keep moving quickly.

All right, Shinigami said enthusiastically after not too long. *Found the systems, and I'm getting into them. Oh man, fucking* jackpot. *They're too smart to keep mission briefs, but I have some of his notes and a bunch of messages—so I have names. Lots of names.*

How much longer do you need for the download? Barnabas sounded concerned.

Not too long, Shinigami assured him.

Tafa kept working, trying to hide her smile. She'd offered her help, and she was pulling the job off. She was managing it.

We have an opportunity, Shinigami exclaimed suddenly.

I'm not sure I like the way you say that, Barnabas stated cautiously.

Yeah, I don't blame you. There's a path from here to the committee's main servers. I can get in, and I'm pretty sure I can get a good deal of data, but I don't think I can do it without tripping alarms.

There was a long pause. Tafa found herself frozen, not sure she wanted them to do it. She had secretly envied the others when they talked about their fights. They were so courageous. They did daring things like she was doing now. Part of her wanted to tell Shinigami to do it, and she'd run out of the building if she had to, dodging the Jotun police officers and pulling off the sort of escape she'd seen the others make.

But the very real possibility of danger was making her sick to her stomach.

Gar seemed to understand. *Can we sacrifice the bot?* he asked practically. *That way, Tafa can start for the exit now, and maybe you initiate as she's on her way down. Because she won't be in the room, they won't know to look for her specifically.*

Good idea, Shinigami said. *Tafa, wrap it up. I'll just destroy the bot when we're done.*

Barnabas gave the silent equivalent of a nod, his agreement a quiet impression in their minds, and Tafa put away her tools with shaking fingers. She opened the door and went out into the hallway with a smile to the two guards.

"Are you the ones who sign off on this?" They shook their mechanical heads, and she heaved a sigh. Playing the part was helping her calm down. "All right, well, thanks. I'll see if I can figure out who I'm supposed to talk to. Have a good shift."

They relaxed somewhat, and one of them wished her a good day as well. She made her way back to the lift, fighting the urge to run with every step.

She was halfway down to the main floor when Shinigami said, *I need to start while she's close enough to provide the uplink. Tafa, get ready to move quickly. If you have to, run, and don't stop when you get outside. Gar and I will take care of things if we need to. We're right there.*

Okay. Tafa stared at the wall and concentrated on not throwing up.

She was halfway down the long corridor to the outside when alarms went off. Luckily, she wasn't the only one who started violently. Several Jotuns looked around, and another Yofu in the corridor clapped his hands over his ears.

"What's that alarm?" Tafa yelled at him as if every part of her wasn't screaming for her to run.

"I don't know," he called back. They were leaning close together, and Tafa could only hope that she seemed to be half of a pair of Yofu, not the single one who'd gone up to Biset's offices.

Tafa shrugged, waved at him, and headed out. There was yelling and Senate police were running all over the place, so she flattened herself against the wall to let them past.

You're a natural, Shinigami told Tafa approvingly. *Now*

get moving. They're getting close to his office, and it's dollars to donuts that those two guards will tell them about you.

I don't know what either of those things is.

We'll work on that in a few minutes. Just go!

Tafa sped up slightly and swallowed hard as she slipped past the last two guards and turned onto the street. No one called after her, though, and a few minutes later, she was practically running across the landing bay to the *Shinigami's* shuttle while Barnabas beckoned and Gar gave her a huge grin.

All three of them went sprawling as Shinigami took the controls and accelerated away at high speed.

"Shinigami," Barnabas said, from the floor, "why—"

"Because they're locking down *everything*." Shinigami looked over her shoulder as the shuttle banked. "But I got their data, and we are good to go. Three cheers for our newest little con artist!"

"Hip, hip, huzzah," Gar said, pulling Tafa to her feet and giving her a hug. "You did it!"

"And now she gets a donut," Shinigami said. *"Everyone* should know about donuts. To a Federation outpost!"

CHAPTER EIGHT

"*What?*" Grisor swung around in his suit to stare at his aide. "*What* did you say?"

"I said, uh..." The aide was fluttering from side to side in his tank, entirely unable to contain his distress. Eventually, he said, "Someone broke into Biset's office, and may have—ah—probably did—ah—use Biset's computers to reach the main committee servers."

The aide's suit was rigid and unmoving. He was clearly consumed with fear, and it took all of Grisor's self-control not to unleash his rage at this very conveniently-placed target.

For he was *consumed* with rage. He had ordered Biset's offices sealed the moment he had learned of the senator's death. So far, they'd managed to keep a lid on things—unlike with Huword, whose death had touched off a storm in the Senate and Navy alike. They didn't need anyone looking closer at Biset and his activities.

But *no one* should have gotten into those offices, and

certainly, no one should have gotten into the committee's servers.

Because the committee should not *have* servers. Had Grisor controlled the kill switches in his fellow committee members' suits, he might well have used every single one of them at that moment. He did not particularly care which of them was responsible for this. He'd always known he was going to have to eliminate most of them at the end, of course, and it was close enough to the end that they would serve little further use.

All that mattered was that one of them had been unforgivably stupid, and now *someone* knew about it.

Grisor forced himself to behave calmly. He did not intend to be the employer aides feared for his temper. That was the mark of a lesser leader. Those who indulged in petty cruelties showed a lack of self-control.

Grisor, meanwhile, held self-control to be the highest virtue.

"The offices were sealed, yes?" He kept his voice quiet.

"Yes, Excellency." The aide seemed worried but was happy to explain. "There were two guards at the door at all times."

"How did someone get into the offices, then?"

"There was, ah—there was a mechanic, sir. An electrical engineer. A Yofu." The aide seemed at once more confident, what with facts to share, and nervous about the information he was imparting. "The Yofu told them that she'd been sent to cut off certain circuits and make sure the systems couldn't be accessed."

Grisor stared at him wordlessly.

"So they let her in," the aide finished lamely, as though he were aware just how much anger this would cause.

"Have they been dealt with?" Grisor asked precisely.

"I...don't know, Excellency."

Calm. He must be calm. The guards would be dealt with soon. Grisor did not indulge in unpredictable violence, but he *did* punish mistakes. His underlings must know the cost of failure, and in this case...there was only one possible price to pay.

He briefly considered killing the guards' families as well but decided against it. That was the sort of thing that might discourage people from serving him.

"So this Yofu accessed Biset's computer systems?"

"Yes, Excellency. They're still trying to determine *how.* It doesn't appear that she did anything other than what she said she was doing. She worked on the two panels she specified to the guards." The aide paused. "It-it *could* be unrelated," he said finally.

"It's *not* unrelated," Grisor stated precisely. "A Yofu, a single Yofu, came into the Senate building, got through security—"

"She didn't go through security, sir. She took one of the lifts. We reviewed the tapes."

"She shouldn't have been able to access the lifts," Grisor said. He was getting tired of pointing out the obvious. "She got into the building, did something she should not be able to do, and was in Biset's office during the data breach."

"Actually, she wasn't, Excellency. She had left by then."

Grisor looked at the aide, who looked back without any trace of guile. As far as Grisor could tell the aide wasn't lying, and he also wasn't stupid. Grisor didn't employ stupid people. It was enough to make Grisor doubt, if just for a moment. Could he be wrong? Was it possible that this Yofu had somehow—

No, it wasn't. Someone knew Biset was dead. Someone had come for his data specifically and had managed to get access to servers that should not even exist.

Grisor stared at the aide a moment longer. "You may go," he said finally. "Tell the committee I wish to address them."

"Yes, Excellency." The aide left so quickly that his suit nearly stumbled over its own feet.

Alone in his office, Grisor wished that he was still incandescently angry. If he were angry, he would be cushioned somewhat against the truly frightening possibility of failure.

The rest of the Senate did not know about the Committee's objectives. Grisor had been careful to maintain secrecy from the start. He knew enough to fear that if word got out, he would be stopped somehow.

It was too early for them to make their move. They knew how to make any mind their own, but the process was slow and required specialized equipment. They still did not have the ability to turn multitudes to their side. That would come when they controlled the Navy and the Senate.

If the Jotun people learned about the Committee now, they would demand that it be closed down. The element of surprise would be entirely gone.

They had to move quickly. Grisor went to his desk and connected a call. He bobbed in the water with impatience as it connected, and finally opened to show one of his guards, left behind at the research facility,

"I need an update," Grisor said abruptly.

"Yes, Excellency," said Feword. His tone was, as always, mild and respectful. It belied his true nature as an individual who killed without hesitation, and with astonishing violence. He had been invaluable to Grisor over the years, not only for that but for his constant attention to detail. "The scientists almost do not rest. They move between their experiments, and often check on Captain Jeltor's progress."

"He is still not converted?" Grisor knew that they would have contacted him with such a development, but he was still disappointed. "Discouraging."

"Yes, Excellency." He paused. "I think it worries them," he said finally. "But that is a guess. They do not spend time speaking with us."

"You think they fear that he will not be converted?" Grisor asked.

"I cannot say, Excellency. It was only a guess. Unlike others that we see often, I do not know them well enough to say with confidence."

"Nevertheless," Grisor said absently, "I trust your judgment. Give them whatever help you can. If he is missing for too much longer, people will start asking questions."

"Yes, Excellency." Feword nodded deeply and held the pose until Grisor cut the call.

Gil and Wev were hard at work in the lab when they heard footsteps.

They did not look at one another. Since they received word of Grisor's imminent arrival, they had behaved as if every interaction could be seen and heard. They were neither foolish nor sloppy; as soon as they arrived, they had disabled the security cameras and set them to display looped videos. Still, they had gotten this far in the JIIA by being exceedingly and relentlessly careful.

One guard or two? Wev asked now.

Gil, who was closer to the door, attuned his auditory implants. *One.*

Both of them readied their weapons. They had always known it might come to a fight. It was not a matter of courage against cowardice. They must defend themselves if they hoped to further their goal.

When the guard appeared in the doorway, both of them gave him respectful nods. So far, the guards had done regular rounds of the building—a nuisance—but had not gotten in their way.

"I have spoken to His Excellency," said the guard, whom Gil recognized as Feword. He seemed to be in charge of the others, although they displayed no ranks on their suits.

Wev, in a rare moment of emotion, said, *Does he mean to be an emperor with that title?*

Yes, Gil replied simply. He looked at Feword. "His Excellency is, perhaps, displeased with us?" He kept his tone respectful and hoped that he seemed appropriately disappointed in himself.

"He is understanding," Feword said. "He knows that your task is difficult. He asked me only to aid you in whatever way you wish." He paused. "Time is of the essence, as you must know. I do not say this to worry you."

That was unexpectedly kind, and Gil reflected that it would be a shame to kill Feword—which, of course, they would inevitably have to do. As far as he could tell the guard was being sincere, both about Grisor's attitude and the offer of help. He did not seem to resent being asked to do this.

Which presented the problem of what they should ask him to do. After all, their main goal each day was to stay busy in a way that cloaked their true inactivity. Under the constant threat of surveillance, they did not dare speak openly to Jeltor or take him out of his tank—and, indeed, they caused him pain because anyone watching would be sure to notice if he was not being hurt. But they were careful not to play the indoctrination tapes, and not to use the mix of chemicals that had been used by the scientists.

Gil made a calculation in his head. Where would the guards be least in the way—and least likely to see something they shouldn't? "It would help us," he said finally, "if you could attend to the other experiments sometimes. With time being a limiting factor, we should devote all our attention to Captain Jeltor."

"We should pause the other experiments," Wev concurred, picking up the thread. "You would need only to provide them with food."

Feword nodded. "We will wait for you to show us the procedures."

"I will go," Wev said to Gil. "I think, perhaps, a bit more intensity in the solution." He led the way out of the laboratory, and Feword nodded to Gil before following.

Alone now—or, at least, alone in terms of sentient companions—Gil went to the tank and stared at Jeltor. The longer this charade went on as he and Wev struggled to find out anything they could about the Committee, the more danger there was that Jeltor's mind would truly break.

Gil watched the senseless Jotun in front of him. If Jeltor must be sacrificed, so be it. Better he break than the committee go unpunished.

And better he break than become a tool for them to use against the Navy.

CHAPTER NINE

Barnabas found Shinigami curled up with a mug of tea, scrolling manually through the data and—as far as he could tell—looking at it with her body's eyes.

Of course, she was scrolling through it at a speed that made his eyes water. And she'd forgotten to put a tea bag in the hot water. And she was wearing fuzzy socks and a hoodie with a nightgown that probably shouldn't be worn in this setting. But she was trying to get used to doing things, and he grinned at her as he came over to sit.

"Should I have worn my pajamas?" he asked lightly.

"Are these pajamas?" Shinigami asked. "The socks are slippery. That would make sense."

"They're not strictly... Uh, where did you get the nightgown?"

"Tabitha left it."

Barnabas resisted the urge to gouge his eyes out, which he told himself would not work with a mental image. Tabitha was a very attractive woman, but he'd always viewed her as more like a niece—and on an equivalent level to a toddler, given her penchant for getting into extraordinarily dangerous situations and then being stubborn about following advice to get out of them.

"It's not the sort of thing most people would wear in public," he said finally.

"I'm pretty sure this is *less* revealing than things a lot of people wear to go out to breakfast these days," Shinigami said in deep amusement.

"Where in God's name have you been eating breakfast?"

"Not the point. But I'll change and wear a flannel nightshirt if it would make you more comfortable."

"No, no, don't go to any trouble." Barnabas squinted at the screen. "I'll just look in this direction."

Shinigami snickered. "God help you the first time a woman tries to make a pass at you. Come to think of it, God help *her*, getting mixed up with you."

"Women don't make passes at me," Barnabas replied idly. "Which is good."

He thought briefly of Sarah and her son. It was clear that Sarah had harbored tentative hopes that Barnabas might make a good husband and father. Neither of them, however, had truly wanted that, so they had drifted their separate ways amicably. The last Barnabas had heard, she had settled on High Tortuga and was married now.

Not eager to have his romantic life dredged up as a topic of discussion, he nodded at the screen. "So, what have you found?"

"So much," Shinigami said. "Unfortunately, no one thought to send messages like, 'We shall meet in the grove at midnight,' so I'm just trying to piece together what all this nonsense *means*."

"It would probably help if you didn't think of it as nonsense."

"It *is* nonsense. It's some ridiculous plan to rule the whole universe—*somehow*—and I cannot for the life of me understand why they'd want to. They should talk to Bethany Anne about having power. Actually, come to think of it, that might not be a bad strategy, here."

Barnabas snickered. "What are you thinking? A sit-down tea, or…"

"Just have her explain that being in power is a miserable thing, and then, if they don't listen, she can kill all of them."

"Well, your plans are decisive, I'll give you that. But, just to play devil's advocate, if we *couldn't* get Bethany Anne for this—"

"Yeah, yeah, I know. We're on our own." Shinigami waved her hands and managed to get water all over her socks and the carpet. "Crap. I'll clean that up later."

"Mmm." Barnabas sat back.

"Here's what we know so far," Shinigami said. "It's something to do with mind control in some way. I don't know precisely what they're doing."

"Subliminal commands? Conditioning?" Barnabas frowned. On Earth, Stephen and Jennifer had run into a nasty piece of work who was intending to use mind-controlled Wechselbalg to take over the world.

"Conditioning, I think." Shinigami shook her head. "What I mean is, I'm not sure what they're *going* for. Before you ask, yes, I did look through the files from Stephen's mission, and I don't think it's like that. It seems to be gentler, at least in some ways."

Barnabas raised an eyebrow.

"What was done to the Wechselbalg wasn't intended to make them functional members of society," Shinigami explained. "It was meant to make them into an army. I doubt Hugo even had a plan for them once he'd used them to take over. But this—I honestly think they're trying to deploy it against people who will keep having to be politicians or whatever."

"Manchurian Candidate?" Barnabas queried.

There was a pause while Shinigami looked up the reference. "Maybe," she said. "I don't know, that's the thing. They seem to be intending to deploy it on a broad scale, but think of the processing capability it would take to control that many people."

"Only an AI would say it like that." Barnabas considered. "We should ask Jeltor, you know. There's a chance that someone has tried this before, and he might know of it. It might not even have the negative implications it has for us. It's impossible to know."

"Actually, I did send him a message." Shinigami was frowning. "He hasn't responded yet. I know he was meeting with the admiral, and I thought we might get word from him when we were in Hevarod. We left so quickly, though, and I don't have any idea where he's been since the meeting."

"Huh." Barnabas frowned. "Send a message to her, will you? Ask her if she had a timeline for when he'd be back in contact. No—send a message to Yojira." Jeltor's wife was still in a safe house with their children. "For all we know, he's gone there, and there's nothing to worry about."

"If he were there, he would have gotten my message," Shinigami pointed out. "I'll send a message to make sure everything's fine at the safe house, but I'm also going to send a message to Admiral Jeqwar. You don't get worried for no reason, and you're worried."

"We're up against an enemy I don't understand," Barnabas murmured. "Of course, I'm worried." He rubbed his eyes. "So they want to use mind-control against their own people?"

"I've been thinking about that," Shinigami said. "Yes, *but.*" She paused significantly. "Huword was involved in abducting civilians from many different species, yes? Perhaps he was getting test subjects."

"What's the *goal*?" Barnabas flung himself out of the chair and began to pace.

"Power," Shinigami said immediately. "It's always power with these people."

"They want power, they want— Well, it would have to be mind control, wouldn't it? They'd have to take over other species by warping their minds." Barnabas snorted. "The Navy certainly won't help them."

Both of them realized the truth a moment later.

"Oh, my *God*," Barnabas whispered softly. Old habits died hard, so he did not blaspheme lightly, but right now he was too shocked to do otherwise. "They're going to mind-control the Navy." He had to say it. If he said it, then it would be real, and he would have to deal with it.

Shinigami sat in slack-jawed silence. "They're going to mind-control the Navy," she repeated finally, "and then take over other worlds, mind-controlling the governments and civilians as necessary to keep them in power."

"And once enough people are their slaves, it will be impossible to overthrow them. They'll have turned every one of those people into living shields." Barnabas found that he had the distinct urge to put his fist through a wall. "Son of a *bitch*. Every time I think people can't set the bar any lower…"

"No kidding." It was quite a commentary on their present situation that Shinigami did not seem at all flippant, only stunned. "We have to tell the Navy."

"At once," Barnabas said. "But we have to make sure we get it only to… I don't even know, actually. Is it better to have it go broad and risk tipping them off that we know, or to go targeted and risk getting someone they've already controlled?"

"Jeltor will know," Shinigami said.

"If we get in touch with him soon enough. No, we can't wait." Barnabas went to a cabinet on the side of the room and pulled out a pen and paper. "I'll start drafting something." He saw her raised eyebrow and shrugged. "A pen and paper help me organize my thoughts, and if ever I needed them organized, it's now."

He wrote for a while, struggling to convey everything he knew and how he knew it. Admiral Jeqwar was eminently practical and would hesitate to accuse sitting senators of something like this without good cause. Barnabas knew he did not need ironclad proof, but he *did* need this to sound like something more than a madman's ramblings.

When he looked up, Shinigami had come to join him. She looked at the note and nodded.

"It's good. Should I send it?"

"To whom, though?" Barnabas folded his arms and stared at it. "All of the admirals?"

"Yes." Shinigami nodded. "They'll have to act if it's all of them, won't they?"

"I should hope so, but I'm learning not to put much stock into my assumptions."

"Don't get all grumpy." She smiled at him. "There, I sent it. And remember, when Jeltor found out about the Yennai Corporation, he came with us. So did the entire Navy. This committee is looking at mind-controlling the entire populace. That means the Jotuns aren't what you fear. They're what you *need*."

Barnabas gave her a curious look. "I hadn't thought of it that way."

"For someone who used to spend most of his time thinking about things, you can be... What's the word I'm looking for?"

"Hasty?"

"A less priggish word."

Barnabas laughed. "Come on. Let's go spar—but, please, change first."

Shinigami laughed. "Okay, okay, I get the point—this isn't something you wear outside."

"It really isn't. What would possess you to wear Tabitha's clothes?"

"She wears leather pants all the time. They're shiny, this is shiny; they're tight, this is tight."

"All right, you do actually have logic on your side," Barnabas conceded. "I didn't expect that."

"See? Uh, don't tell Bethany Anne, though."

"I won't if you don't tell Tabitha. She would think it was far too funny."

"Deal."

They shook on it and went to prepare for sparring, but although Barnabas tried to keep his mind on their light conversation, he could not help but dwell on what they'd learned.

What they *suspected*. He reminded himself that there wasn't any proof yet. He was desperately hoping that Admiral Jeqwar would write back and tell him that his fears were unfounded.

They might be, after all, mightn't they? Barnabas could be entirely wrong, as could Shinigami—although the likelihood of that, with the sheer amount of data she'd stored, was vanishingly small. If she thought he was right about this, he probably was.

Which was hardly what he wanted at this juncture. His mind could hardly encompass a scheme of this magnitude. He'd known of the Kurtherians' schemes, of course, and they were certainly far-reaching...but those were imperial ambitions of a sort he recognized. The Kurtherians—some of them, anyway—wanted to conquer.

The Jotuns wanted to take the minds of the people by force.

Barnabas shuddered, then pushed himself up from his seat and changed his clothes quickly. He had to stay in motion and allow the small rituals to free him or he would be lost to worry.

They would expose this. The Jotuns, as Shinigami had pointed out, were not the Committee's allies. They would stand against their Senate, and the universe would see the truth.

It was simply a matter of making sure that happened before there was bloodshed.

CHAPTER TEN

On her first full day aboard the *Palpari*, Aliana made a simple request of Zinqued: give her all of the information you already have on Barnabas and the *Shinigami*, including its crew.

To his credit, he'd done so promptly. The sheer *amount* of information, however, was staggering. He didn't know much about the inner workings of the Empire, but he knew a great deal about the missions Barnabas had completed since he'd come to this sector.

As far as his crew went, there was only one confirmed member: Venfaldri Gar, a Luvendi who had apparently been Barnabas' enemy on High Tortuga—or Devon, as aliens still called it—but was now a trusted friend. Aliana chewed her lip as she considered that. She supposed perhaps she could work her way onto the *Shinigami's* crew, but she'd need to learn more about Barnabas before she felt comfortable doing that.

What was interesting was that Gar had been a member

of a mining syndicate, and had therefore participated in something very close to slavery. Probably, he had participated in something that *was* slavery in all but name. Aliana knew the stories of what had happened on High Tortuga, and she was sure that a lot of people had found themselves trapped in illegal "contracts" with no real means of escape.

Zinqued was not exactly sure what had happened on High Tortuga. After all, there were stringent requirements for ships to dock on the planet, and ships with all the hallmarks of pirates weren't going to be allowed, the new name of the planet notwithstanding. In fact, Zinqued really shouldn't know about the planet. The Empire had made sure to erase most references to it from galactic directories and to spread false stories about hard crop yields and empty mines.

All Zinqued knew, therefore, was that the sole crew member was Venfaldri Gar, who had once been employed by a mining syndicate Barnabas had eliminated in a fairly dramatic fashion.

This left Aliana filling in the blanks on her own, and she couldn't help but wonder if there was any way *she* could find out more details. She was human, after all, and maybe…well, maybe she knew someone who could tell her details. She was absolutely, definitively *not* going to go to a human outpost. She wasn't in the mood for either guilt trips or Lawrence.

She deliberated over a few cups of tea before finally deciding to go for it and typed out a message to her Uncle Carter. She asked him if he had any connections on High Tortuga, since she was chasing down some rumors about a mine on the planet's smaller continent.

She felt comfortable contacting him, at least. The last she'd heard, he and his wife Elisa were roaming around with no intentions of having any children, and the whole family was shaking their heads over it. It meant that Aliana's decision to head out was, if not understood and respected, at least not unprecedented.

She felt a little guilty at the thought of Carter getting angry messages from her parents, though. She remembered them yelling at her and her yelling back, "Uncle Carter is off seeing the universe, why can't I?"

The memory was enough to make her cringe. Was there anyone, she wondered, who *didn't* look back at their younger self and want to sink through the floor with embarrassment?

Her message sent, she looked up details on more recent missions undertaken by the *Shinigami*. Apparently, after High Tortuga, Barnabas and his very small crew had managed to take down a mercenary company, which by itself would have been impressive, but they had then gone on to destroy the parent corporation as well. Aliana had never heard of the Yennai Corporation, but when she did a little bit of digging on its subsidiaries, she found herself staring at the screen in awe.

It seemed like they'd owned half the sector, if not more —and it had taken the Jotun Navy to back Barnabas up with enough strength to destroy them.

Because they had their own fleet.

This was insane. It really *was* the Wild West out here, as Uncle Carter liked to call it. Aliana had grown up using the term, although she had only the vaguest idea of what it meant, having been born and raised on the *Meredith Reynolds.*

Thinking of the *Meredith Reynolds,* however, made her think of—

No. Those memories were worse than the memories of Lawrence. Aliana looked bitterly at her tea and wished it was something that would help her stop thinking entirely. Straight vodka, maybe.

She went back to reading, but it provided no escape. The more she read, the more Aliana became convinced that this plan of Zinqued's was impossible. The things that made the *Shinigami* such an attractive ship were exactly the things that made it nigh-impossible to steal: its speed and maneuverability, its weapons, and its AI.

She was fascinated by the AI. She'd never met one, but she'd heard the stories of course. ArchAngel was a legend. What was this one like? Very cold and emotionless, she supposed. It *was* a computer, after all. She could imagine it having been programmed to say please and thank you all the time, and being very stuffy when people were rude to it.

Had Shinigami or Barnabas heard these internal thoughts, they would have laughed themselves sick.

She had finished her latest batch of documents and was tipped back in her chair studying the ceiling when Zinqued came to find her.

"Hello," he said from the doorway.

Aliana swore and nearly went over backward. She apologized as she righted the chair and stood up awkwardly. She might abhor politeness, but it was drilled into her.

"Please don't be so formal." Zinqued gave her an easy

smile. "I haven't been a captain for very long, so it still seems odd to have people stand. In any case, I don't care about those things."

Aliana smiled. She really did like this Hieto. Some captains were absolutely determined to snatch every bit of respect they felt the universe owed them, and that made them completely insufferable. Working for one of those was a nightmare—they wanted their crew to stave off the truth that the universe was a vast, uncaring place and they really weren't important at all.

Zinqued seemed to accept this cheerfully if he thought of it at all. Aliana suspected that he would only shrug if she mentioned it.

"How is everything going?" Zinqued asked her.

"Ah…" Aliana froze. "Well…" How on Earth was she going to tell him what she had learned?

"Not so well, then?" Zinqued asked shrewdly.

"Um. Not yet." She looked at the tablet and back at him. "I'm sorry. I've sent a message to my uncle to see if he can tell us any more stories about Barnabas, but right now, this ship looks like it's going to be difficult to take. I really don't know how we're going to pull it off."

"I know." Zinqued didn't seem at all worried. "I hoped you would say that."

"Excuse me?" Maybe she had this all wrong, and he was as crazy as a loon.

"If you'd told me it was going well, I'd have to think you were lying to me," he explained. "We came up with several good plans that failed in practice. Too much confidence would be a bad sign, but you were honest that you don't know how to do this."

"I read up on those other plans." Since he wasn't going to be offended, Aliana sat back down. "With Empire technology being what it is, I'm not sure how successful anything like that will be. I think we can't expect to steal the ship in a normal way. We have to trick them into giving it to us somehow."

Zinqued gave a hearty laugh. "Aha! The human is trickier than we are. I look forward to seeing how you pull that off."

"Er…" She took a sip of cold tea. "Right. And you'll want to be careful of the AI. It makes the ship into a weapon, and I wouldn't bet you could deactivate it."

Zinqued tilted his head to the side curiously.

"What do you know of the Empire's AIs?" Aliana asked.

"I know they are powerful computers."

"They're aware," Aliana explained. "Sentient. *Truly* sentient. And, as you say, they are powerful. This one controls that ship. If you've ever heard stories of—" She broke off when the captain's face went pale. "What is it?"

"Tik'ta told a story," he said slowly. "The ship used its doors to kill a member of her crew before Barnabas killed her first captain. They thought the other crew member had commanded the ship to use the doors that way, but what if it was the ship? I did not know it could protect itself that way."

"Oh, it can," Aliana said. "If this ship really has an AI, and it seems like it does, you're in for a world of hurt if you don't account for that somehow."

"How do we do that?" Zinqued asked at once.

"I…don't know." Aliana grimaced. "We're going to need

to pull off one of the best cons in history to do this, and I'm not a conwoman."

"What is a 'con?'"

"It's...um, a scheme, I guess. You use lies and tricks to fool people into doing things." Aliana considered. "Often people will steal things doing that. They would maybe dress up as police officers and pretend there was a problem with a bank, and then steal the money."

"Ah," Zinqued murmured in understanding.

"But they're a *lot* more complicated than that," Aliana hastened to explain. "Really. Honestly. And I don't really know how to pull one off."

"Then you will figure it out, eh?" Zinqued apparently had no worries on that front.

Tik'ta might be right about all this, Aliana thought. Zinqued didn't seem to have his head screwed on straight when it came to this ship.

Her monitor dinged and she leaned in to look, only to make a sound of surprise. "Holy crap. All right, there's a stroke of luck." She smiled up at Zinqued. "My Uncle Carter lives on High Tortuga now, apparently. He owns a bar." That *did* sound like him. "I was vague, I just asked about an incident with a mine on the smaller continent, and he says he thinks he knows what I'm talking about, and he *does* know what happened there. If we want to find out more about Barnabas, that's the way to go."

"Will we get clearance to land on High Tortuga?" Zinqued asked in surprise.

"He says so. Said to reference him and gave us a pass." Aliana smiled. "I guess we're going to High Tortuga. Well, if you don't have anywhere else to go."

"We would need to pay for fuel to get there," Zinqued pointed out.

"Oh. Hmm. I'll ask if we can courier anything in. We'll figure it out. There's always a way to make money on the way to somewhere," Aliana said.

"Or while we're there." Zinqued's smile was a bit too sly.

"I wouldn't try that," Aliana told him bluntly. "You think *Barnabas* is scary? You haven't met Bethany Anne. And if you cause shit on *her* planet, you're gonna learn *all* about her."

"Ah. That is good to know. I will tell Tik'ta to make the preparations."

CHAPTER ELEVEN

It was late when Carter closed up Aebura's Bar and headed upstairs to the apartments on the third floor. He walked carefully to avoid making any of the floorboards squeak, and took special care as he snuck past the twins' room.

He should probably fix the floorboards, but he really didn't mind the way they squeaked or their rough appearance. When Aebura had built the bar, she'd made the upstairs apartments suitable for Ubuara, so Carter had needed to make them over. While there were still some tunnels for the twins to crawl around in, he'd managed to make proper rooms and corridors with scrap wood from other construction in Tethra.

He loved the result, squeaking floors and all. He loved that he could *see* his handiwork in each board and nail. He had spent decades on the *Meredith Reynolds*, not to mention various Empire ships, and while he loved their sleek look, he was much more suited to log cabins and chopping firewood.

He'd built this place. His children were sleeping in beds he'd crafted, in a room he'd built painstakingly by hand, above the bar he ran, a place full of friends and stories. He wouldn't trade any of this for the world.

To his surprise, there was a light under the bedroom door, and he slipped into the master bedroom to find Elisa still up.

"What are you doing awake? It's late."

"And hello to you, too." She smiled up at him and turned her head so that he could drop a kiss on her cheek. "Unfortunately, I've been losing my dinner. I don't remember being this sick when I was pregnant with the twins."

Carter felt a pang of worry and tried to mask it, stripping off his work clothes and dropping them in the hamper. "Maybe it's different every time."

"I think so." When he looked at her, she was smiling contentedly, not at all worried. "The doctor said a lot of nausea is a good sign, actually."

"Good for who?" Carter demanded.

She laughed. "I know. I strongly considered throwing up on him." She set the book she'd been reading on her stomach and nodded at the computer. "I stayed up partially because you got a message from Aliana, and I wanted to make sure you saw it. She says she'll be here in a couple of days on a ship called the *Palpari*. She sent the make and details."

"That's great!" Carter, despite himself, felt a surge of relief. "I sent the invitation, but I wasn't sure she'd actually come."

"You're worried about her." Elisa sounded surprised. "You don't get worried often. Are things not working between her and Lawrence, then?"

Her voice held reserve—as well it might, Carter thought. None of the family liked Lawrence. They hadn't exactly been subtle about it, either, and Aliana had responded by cutting *them* off instead of him.

Carter tended to think his family was more than a little overbearing and meddlesome, and he'd always been one of the black sheep. However lovingly his parents, aunts, and uncles got on his case about his travels and wild ways, they really did mean what they said—they wished he would settle down somewhere normal and have a simple life.

Really, he was as surprised as anyone to find himself here now, a family man with a small business, his feet firmly planted in one place. It was just far enough off the map that his parents could still complain, but still adventurous enough for him.

In Aliana's case, though, he almost thought the family hadn't gone far enough. Aliana had found Lawrence so quickly after tragedy struck that it was hard not to think she was simply trying to forget her pain.

And Lawrence...

"Lawrence is a rat bastard," Carter told Elisa as he pulled on an old t-shirt and some flannel pants, "but I think the only way we'll keep Aliana around long enough that she'll start to trust us is if we don't get on his case."

Elisa dropped her head back against the headboard and groaned. "You know I hate that, right? We spent all those years on other people's ships, and now we finally have our own house. No one should be allowed to be a rat bastard to us in our own house!"

Carter had to admit she had a point with that one. "Well, if he decides to come after the kids—"

"If he comes after the kids, I'm gonna mama bear his ass into the ground," Elisa growled. Her tone was unequivocal enough that Carter felt the urge to put on some body armor—just in case the mama bear came out while he was around.

He smiled, though, and got into bed beside her. "Will I be allowed to get a punch in?"

"Maybe." She flashed her dimple at him when she grinned. "I love you a lot, but I'll have to decide if I love you *that* much."

"Oh! That's how we're playing?"

Elisa laughed as she put her book on the side table and nestled against him. "So, why did Aliana write to you? You never said."

"Ah, right." Carter wrapped his arm around her. "It's the funniest thing. She wrote me to ask if I knew anything about a mine that had been liberated on the smaller continent."

"*Wait.*" Elisa sat upright and stared at him. "You mean—"

"Yeah. I don't know how she even heard about it. Barnabas tracked down everyone who knew..." Carter scratched his head. "Anyway, I wrote out this long message, and then I thought—well, let's see why she wants to know."

He hated to admit it, but with Lawrence in the picture, he didn't entirely trust Aliana's motives. Not that he could think of a bad motive for her wanting to know about it, of course. No matter what Lawrence suggested, Aliana was hardly going to get involved in organized crime or anything like that.

Was she? He lay back, his mind racing.

"You know what you should do," Elisa said sleepily as she cuddled against him. She yawned. "You should invite Barnabas back here to talk to her. If she wants to know about the mines, he could tell her. Besides, he never takes vacations."

"Barnabas," Carter said. His eyes snapped open as he considered.

Yes. That was a very, very good idea. From what Carter had heard, Lawrence was hardly the type to take any other man seriously. Carter could just imagine him superciliously ordering Carter around in his own bar. It was enough to make him want to stab the other man in the face.

But Barnabas...

Barnabas wouldn't stand for any disrespect. He would politely and devastatingly put Lawrence in his place.

"You're a genius," Carter murmured into Elisa's hair and kissed the top of her head. She muttered something sleepy and not quite intelligible, and he smiled as he turned off the light.

Barnabas dipped a brush into ink and drained the excess carefully into the tiny bowl before moving it over a sheet of paper. He lowered it and adjusted his pressure, dragging the brush with exquisite slowness, abandoning the need for quickness and completion.

He cultivated the practice of calligraphy, not the results. He found the slowness of action, the immutability of paper and ink, and the necessity of perfect form and relaxation throughout the whole body calming and centering. Even as a monk, he had found that his most intense prayer came when he was tending the gardens or doing some other work.

He had just completed the second line of an epic poem composed in China's Sui Dynasty when Shinigami rapped on the door.

"Yo, chief."

Barnabas looked over.

"I didn't ruin anything, did I?" Shinigami craned her neck to look at the paper. "I waited until you were done with a line."

"Thank you." Barnabas smiled. Once that sort of thoughtfulness would have been totally alien to Shinigami. "What can I help with?"

"You got a message from Carter, actually." Shinigami leaned in the doorway, arms crossed. "Don't worry, nothing urgent. He wants you to come meet his niece, apparently?"

"I'm sorry, *what?*"

"That was my reaction, too."

"Let's skip past the part where you read my messages," Barnabas said wearily. "Why does he want me to meet this woman?"

"He's being cagey," Shinigami replied. "He said she wanted to know about the mine, but there's clearly some subtext. Something about not liking... I don't know, he wants us to go to Tethra and meet her."

"Huh." Barnabas considered this. He looked at his calligraphy. He looked out the window. "No word from Jeltor yet, I take it. Or Admiral Jeqwar."

"No," Shinigami told him quietly. "I'd have told you at once."

"I know. I was just..." Barnabas rubbed at his face. "I was just hoping," he said quietly. He knew it was illogical, but he could not stop hoping to hear something. The longer they went without word from Jeltor, the more worried he got.

Shinigami said nothing. She was looking away, concern plain on her face.

Barnabas sighed and put down the brush. "Right. I'll, uh... Tell Carter we'll be there when we can." He caught sight of Shinigami's face. "What?"

"We could go now," she suggested.

"We're in the middle of what's probably going to be a war," Barnabas stated brutally.

"Not *yet*, but we're going to be." She came to lean on his desk and looked him in the eye. "Once the fleets start moving, how much free time do you think we'll have? And...well, anything involving fleets is risky. Do you really want to sit here and think about Jeltor being missing or do you want to go spend some time with friends?"

Barnabas looked at her and heaved another sigh. "You know, I think I liked it better before you got a handle on human nature. Now you're far too perceptive." He smiled at her and stood. "You're right. I'll write back to Carter and tell him we're on our way. I can ask him if Elisa needs anything."

"You're such a worrier," Shinigami commented, rolling her eyes. "Elisa is on High Tortuga. At worst, she's going to need something sent over from the main continent, and you know Tabitha will take on delivery duties all day long if she gets a sandwich out of the deal."

"Good point." Barnabas led the way into the hall. "Okay, so tell me what Carter's message said *exactly*?"

"He said his niece was coming, and that he'd appreciate your presence to 'enforce good manners.' I guess she wants to know about the mine, and... You know, he was talking in circles."

"You're sure this isn't just you failing to understand colloquialisms?"

"You're hardly the person to help with that—as evidenced by the fact that you're calling them 'collo-quialisms.'"

"That's the correct term," Barnabas argued.

"Uh-huh. So, should I just tell him we're on our way? We're a couple of days out, assuming we don't burn the engines too hard. Well, maybe we should. I don't know when shit's going to kick off."

"Are you kidding? Helen would murder us." The mechanic on Federation Border Station 7 had not been a fan of the way Barnabas kept up the *Shinigami*. She'd given him strict instructions to bring the ship in every two months, a recommendation she'd qualified with, "or every two weeks given how you seem to fly it, hot rod."

Barnabas was many centuries old, a vampire, and had

been one of the highest-ranking members of the Etheric Empire, and he still didn't want to cross her.

Shinigami snickered but peeled off to the bridge and let Barnabas head to his quarters to compose a message.

Carter—

It will be good to see you, although I admit I have some trepidation regarding the mention of manners. Regardless, I will be glad to see you and Elisa, and I am looking forward to meeting your niece.

Sincerely, Barnabas

CHAPTER TWELVE

In the research station on Gokrun III, not too far from the now-flooded and defunct robotics factory Barnabas had destroyed, Wev leaned close to his screen and focused on sliding tiny packets of data into the outgoing server traffic.

The research station had been locked down by someone who was both very good at data security and very paranoid. Wev supposed this was probably a good quality in someone who was trying to take over the sector by nefarious means, but it was presently an inconvenience to him.

Sensing how imminent the Committee's plans were, Gil and Wev had sped up their timeline. They were beginning to send data back to the Jotun Interplanetary Intelligence Agency. They had sent an overview of the entire plan and were now backing up all of the data they could get their tentacles on.

They were hampered by two things. First, the data

security practices, which strictly controlled the outgoing data and which would also alert some unknown person when the data deviated from expected margins; and, second, the guards Grisor had left, who stuck their noses into things with alarming regularity.

Both Gil and Wev had considered simply leaving—abandoning the experiments to their fate, with the exception of Jeltor, who would probably have to be killed. They could not take the chance of trying to smuggle a third individual out, and he was too dangerous to leave in the clutches of the Committee. Two, however, could probably make it out, and it wasn't out of the question that they could do considerable damage to the equipment while leaving.

But they needed the data. There was no telling who else had the research results from the team here; who could recreate the experiments, given the technology and methodology. Come to think of it, there was no way of knowing who else had the machinery.

So they had to send everything they had and hope that if the Committee unleashed its plan, the JIIA could somehow begin undoing the conversion process.

Wev found the very idea abhorrent, and it was only worse with the term they used: *conversion*. Such a euphemism. They were mind-controlling people, and yet they spoke of it as if they were leading people to a true change of heart instead of torturing them into it.

He wanted nothing more than to subject every member of the committee to this torture as part of their punishment. Biset's death had been too quick, and so had Huword's.

"Hello," said a voice from the doorway.

Wev refrained from jumping and composed himself before turning in his suit. "Hello," he said as pleasantly as he could. Both he and Gil had been trained in the minutiae of how to behave "normally"—as if someone was a friend, not an enemy. "Did you rest well?"

"Not so well," Feword admitted. "It is difficult to block out the experiments."

The sounds often kept Wev up as well. The aliens and other Jotuns who had been taken for experimentation had been broken entirely by the torture the original research team put them through. The first attempts to create obedient servants had been unsubtle at best, and many of the aliens bore the scars of old injuries. Their cries of anguish echoed through the halls all day and all night until Wev wondered whether a quick death might not be kinder.

He and Gil had kept the aliens alive for exactly the reasons they had given Grisor: they wanted to know if it was possible to rehabilitate the experiments whose minds had been broken. Of course, once they were rehabilitated, Gil and Wev had no intentions of putting them through the conversion process—but Grisor didn't need to know that.

Wev simply could not bring himself to walk away. Every time he questioned whether death would be kinder than life, he felt a wave of revulsion. Just because they were scared, injured, and mutilated did not mean that they should be killed.

He wanted to try to heal them. He was ill-equipped to do so, not being a doctor—not to mention having a great deal of vital work to do as a spy. He should not be spending his time on a few injured aliens when there were so many others who needed his help.

But their suffering was too much for him to endure without at least *trying* to help them.

He wondered whether Feword's conscience was also troubled by the sounds, or if it was only an inconvenience. Probably, it was simply an inconvenience. Feword struck Wev as an enforcer, his low-key demeanor a mask for easy cruelty. Wev had seen his type before.

So, as pleasant as Feword seemed, he did not relax his vigilance.

"I am sorry there are not more restful quarters," Wev said apologetically. "This must have been an unexpected assignment for you."

Feword bobbed in his tank with faint amusement. "A bit. The committee's work has taken us to many places, but always as His Excellency's guard. Guarding scientists is…different."

"I hope you are not too worried about our safety." Wev tried to keep his voice level, although he felt a stab of alarm. What did Feword mean when he said he was guarding them? "The experiments really are quite contained."

"Ah, that is not what I meant." Feword came closer, and it took all of Wev's self-control not to show his fear. "The longer the experiments go on, especially in the case of the captain—" he used his tentacles to point at Jeltor, "the more chance there is that someone will find the facility and attempt to stop the research."

"Yes," Wev said blankly. "Yes, that's certainly a possibili-ty." He made an attempt to seem worried. "But such things are always a possibility when one pushes the boundaries of science. I try not to trouble myself with them."

Feword bobbed in agreement. "A wise course. His Excellency is much the same. Now, tell me how I may best assist you with these machines? These are the controls for the message, yes? And this is for the chemicals?"

In her private ship at the center of the fleet, Admiral Jeqwar floated in her tank and let her physical body sink into stillness. Her awareness reached out beyond her body until she inhabited the entire ship. Through the sensors built into each component, she could feel the health of the ship.

When a ship was in battle, there was a constant stream of information from all stations, and keeping up with it could be difficult. When not in battle, it was easy to see all of it at once. The scanners gave a faint impression in her mind, showing her each ship in their range like a pinprick of awareness in her physical body. Meanwhile, each battle station hummed quietly, its personal signature well-known to her after so many years.

She took time to inspect the missile and fighter tubes, running faint currents along them. Some had wear and tear on the inside of the tube. It could cause problems in an engagement, so she tagged each affected tube as requiring maintenance.

She moved on to the engines, ignoring the official diagnostic panel and listening to both the engine core and the surrounding structure. It was maintained well by the mechanics, and there were no problems to be found.

In the communications hub, she searched for loose connecting wires and faulty receivers and found a few that would soon need maintenance. She tagged them for her officers to correct; she preferred them to have hands-on experience with the equipment.

Jeqwar was an exacting captain, in part because of her natural affinity for her work. She had never been entirely sure what was missing from her life until she was first plugged into one of the larger ships. Suddenly, her dissatisfaction with both her Jotun body and her biosuit had snapped into focus. In a ship, receiving so much information every second, having so many functions she could control simultaneously, she felt alive in a way she never had before.

For her, it was easy to speak to a ship and have it listen. When a battle began and she took over hundreds of functions simultaneously, she reveled in the challenge.

She passed the point of mere *challenge* when she took control of the whole fleet. She had done so only four times in a true battle, but each had been an experience she could never forget. She *became* the fleet and forgot her small, mortal body entirely. There was no more struggle. Her mind seemed to stretch endlessly to encompass every ally and enemy, every function of every ship.

She craved battle, even though she knew she should not. She should crave peace, shouldn't she? Everyone should; it was simply that she was apparently made for war.

Sometimes the craving for battle was easier to bear, and

sometimes, like now, it was more difficult. Right now, she knew that she craved it for the same reason she was doing all of her maintenance checks on her own instead of having the mechanics do them.

She was worried about Jeltor.

It had not been long since they heard from him. She had not expected much of anything, in fact, for weeks.

But then she had received word from the *Shinigami*. They had not heard from Jeltor either, and she found it unlikely in the extreme that he would go searching for Huword's assassin without them. It had been their crew who found the assassin the first time, tracking her from the Brakalon transport on which Huword had been murdered and following the clues she left to kill Senator Biset.

If Jeltor had not spoken to *them*...

Something had happened to him, and whoever had killed him had kept it quiet, like Huword's death, and Biset's. Jeqwar felt a rising sense of the ridiculous; the Senate and the Navy were prowling around one another, picking off each other's agents, neither admitting what they were doing or even admitting their losses. It was insane.

Someday soon, the Jotun citizens might look up and realize that they had no senators or captains left. Of course, that might not be the worst thing. Jeqwar had to admit that.

She let her consciousness prowl around the ship, circling through each system as though pacing the perimeter of a room.

She had to retrace his steps, she decided, starting from

the moment he had left her sight on Jotuna. She might hit a dead end, but she couldn't give up before she had even started. Whatever had happened, she would find out as much as she could and appeal to Barnabas for help.

She did not like involving other species in Jotun business.

But it seemed she had no choice.

Jeltor floated limply in a haze of pain. It had been days now, or had it been weeks? Or mere minutes? There had been darkness and light by turns, pain and relief, fear and outright terror. He was being tortured, he thought, but they had not asked him any questions.

If they had, he did not remember. What had he said? What had he admitted?

More fear. The only thing he had, the only piece of hope, was that he was still alive. When the pain was at its worst, he knew he had pleaded for them to kill him, but they had not listened.

Whoever they were.

A figure approached the tank. Jeltor could barely see it, the damage to his body was so great, but he saw the shadow and heard the footsteps. A biosuit. Another Jotun.

The tapes started up again. Most of the time they said only nonsense words, although once they had told Jeltor that he must embrace the authority of someone named Grisor. He did not know who Grisor was, and they had never repeated that message.

This time it was something different.

"Captain Jeltor." The voice was very quiet. Like all of the tapes, it reverberated in the water around him. "Maintain your courage. Do not break. There are those here who will help you. I cannot say more."

Jeltor thrashed in the water. *Wait!* He could not make his body work properly, and there seemed to be no hookups to let him speak. Perhaps, he thought bleakly, that was why they had not killed him when he had asked—they could not hear him. *Wait, please! You must say more!*

But there was a click and a moment of white noise, and then the normal tapes resumed with their nonsensical babble.

He had heard it. He *swore* he had heard it.

Hadn't he?

CHAPTER THIRTEEN

"You're freaking kidding me," Aliana said when Carter told her that he and Elisa had children. "*You?*"

"Yes," Carter repeated patiently.

"No, seriously. *You?*"

"You know, I'm beginning to feel a little insulted."

Aliana laughed. "No, it's not that." She gave a shrug as the two of them wove their way through the bustle of Tethra's streets. "It's… I don't know, you were always going to be this bachelor, off living a life of adventure. And then you met Elisa, and it seemed like she was the sort who'd go off and have adventures with you. The idea of you being a respectable businessman, all grounded and…" She waved her hands. "You know, settled down, with kids—"

"Whoa, whoa, whoa." Carter gave her a mock glare that had just the smallest edge to it. "I wouldn't say I'm 'settled down.'"

"You said you've been doing renovations on the apart-ment. You have two kids. Also, judging by the number of people who are waving at you, you're pretty well known around here." Aliana looked around. "Also, this is a *lot* of aliens. I thought High Tortuga was all…human-y."

"The main continent, much more so." Carter smiled to the people around him. "It's one of the reasons I like Tethra so much more, actually. We still have that Wild West feel."

"*There's* the uncle I remember." Aliana grinned at him and elbowed him in the side.

He smiled back at her and confided, "I do like it here. Don't tell my twenty-year-old self. He'd be very disappointed in me, but I'm really enjoying going to sleep in a proper bed each night, knowing the same people will be there when I wake up in the morning. Also, sleeping in a proper bed does wonders for your back."

"Who knew?" Aliana joked. She was smiling easily, happier here than she could remember being for months. The sun was shining, the street was full of amazing smells from the food vendors, and she felt like she could really relax around Carter. Of all her family, he'd been the one who was always there for her—even when he was off adventuring.

She looked at him and saw him watching her.

"How are you?" he asked her quietly.

Aliana swallowed. "I'm fine," she said, turning her head to look at the street. She tried to recapture the ease she'd felt only a few moments before, but even though the sun was still shining and the birds were still chirping, it was gone. "Uh, so you have a lot of monkeys here, huh?"

"Those are Ubuara," Carter said. "And they're intelligent. That's Oemuga there. Wave hello."

Aliana waved, half-expecting that this was going to be

some sort of prank, but to her surprise, the Ubuara who had been loitering on a nearby roof swung down to the street and leapt onto Carter's shoulder.

It chittered at her, and then said in very good English, "I am pleased to meet you. You are Carter's brother-son-daughter?"

"I tried to teach them 'niece' and 'nephew,'" Carter murmured. "It didn't really take. They're obsessed with accuracy, so the term great-niece just has too many unknowns, I guess." He waved his hands and rolled his eyes, but his smile showed that he was just teasing the Ubuara.

"I'm very pleased to meet you, too, Oemuga," Aliana said politely. "It is nice to see where my uncle lives." She traced the relationship in her head and added, "My father-father-brother, I mean."

Oemuga chittered happily. "See?" he asked Carter. "*She* understands." Apparently, he considered the conversation over, since he proceeded to leap back up to the roof with a swish of his tail.

"Well done," Carter murmured, and she heard genuine happiness in his voice. "The Ubuara are sort of...hive-minded? Not quite. They have their own thoughts, but often know each other's. Oemuga likes you, so the rest of them are much more likely to now as well."

Aliana smiled at the Ubuara and gave a little wave as Carter set off again. It wasn't much farther before he led her into an unimpressive building with a wooden sign over the door. Inside, however...

Aliana broke into a grin. If Carter were going to settle down somewhere, it would *absolutely* be somewhere like this. The bar was lovingly tended, its roughly-made furniture carefully smoothed, its floors clean, and with tiny decorative touches that alluded to Carter's years on various spaceships. She saw coins from various planets, little carved statues, postcards, and tiny hanging ornaments.

"Elisa is out with the kids," Carter explained. "Wait here a moment." He went over to the counter and called something through the window. A moment later two sandwiches were handed out, and he piled them onto a tray before taking down two glasses and pouring rich golden beers into them. He jerked his head at a table in the corner, and Aliana practically ran to pull out his chair and take a seat.

"*Beer*," she said. She took a long drink and groaned. "Oh, yeah, that's the stuff. Where'd you get this?"

"BMW. Where else?" Carter smiled. "I got the hookup."

"*How?*" Aliana picked up a sandwich and bit into it. "Holy crap, this is fucking *amazing*. Can I swear? I don't want to swear if your kids might walk in."

"Probably best not to." Carter shrugged. "We've been trying to say things like crap and frack and so on. We haven't been *entirely* successful, mind you, but we're trying."

Aliana grinned and tucked into her food, wolfing it down in time to see another sandwich arrive. She ate that one as well and washed it down with a second beer, and then a third.

"I'm glad I remembered how much you could eat," Carter said affectionately. "Your cousin Mortie, now, we called him a black hole because he was as dumb as a box of rocks. You just eat everything."

"*Everything*," Aliana agreed glumly. She'd often spent a good deal of her limited earnings on extra food when her employers had complained about her raiding the communal kitchen. She was licking her fingers when she saw the look on Carter's face. "Oh, no. No, don't do this. I don't want to talk about it. I told you I'm fine."

"And *I* am your uncle, and I'm worried about you," Carter explained.

"Can't we do this after we talk about the mine prison-break thing?"

"Nope." Carter set down two more mugs of beer. "*Talk.* Tell me how you've been." He seemed to be debating whether or not to ask, but finally did. "Thought you might bring Lawrence."

Aliana had been taking a gulp of beer to steel her nerves. She set the mug back down and looked away.

"Everything all right?" Carter asked.

"No," Aliana said flatly. "It's not, so why don't you just get it out of the way, Uncle Carter?" She knew her voice was bitter, but she didn't think she could make herself sound any more polite. "Why don't you all tell me how you knew he was bad news and I should have listened to everyone?"

There was a long silence, and Carter scooched his chair over next to hers. He leaned back in his seat, rested his feet on the table and his beer on his stomach, and handed her beer back to her. He nodded for her to slouch down too, and she gave a weary laugh when she did.

"I'm not going to say I told you so," Carter began. "I

always hated hearing that. Some mistakes you gotta make. You heard how I nearly wound up dead on an abandoned space station that one time. Uncle Wes—I don't think you've ever met him—had to come bail me out, and my *God* did I get an earful. By the time we were halfway back to Segura Station, I was ready to tell him to put me back where he'd found me."

Aliana looked at him. When he gave her an easy smile, she managed to find a small one of her own.

"What I mean," Carter continued, "is that I had my reasons for making that gamble, and I'm sure you had your reasons for marrying Lawrence."

Aliana groaned and dropped her head back. "It was so stupid of me. It was so fucking *unbelievably* stupid. Ugh. I'm sorry. It was so *freaking* stupid."

"Tell you what, free pass on swearing until we get through this conversation."

"Fuck, yeah." She took a sip of beer.

There was a pause.

"So I take it Lawrence isn't in the picture anymore?" Carter inquired.

"No." Aliana blew out her breath in a sigh. "He married me to get rights to the ship, and then he jacked it, took my crew, and left me with a little deathtrap ship all of his creditors knew about."

"*Oof.*" Carter shook his head. "Son of a bitch. You catch up with him and make his life hell yet?"

"Baby steps." Aliana took another gulp. "I don't want to see him, really."

"Well, I can understand that." Carter rubbed his face.

Aliana rolled her head sideways to look at him. "I know

everyone thought it was dumb to get married so soon after, uh…" She forced herself to say it. "After Harry died." She downed the rest of the beer in a big gulp.

"You miss him," Carter stated neutrally.

"Of course I miss him!" Her voice was too loud, and she wiped her eyes. "I'm sorry. I didn't mean to yell."

"It's okay. I don't mind." He met her eyes.

"Stop looking at me like you pity me."

"Yeah." He nodded. "I can see how that would…yeah. You left so quickly, though, after everything. Was there anything we could have done to make it—I don't know, suck less?"

Aliana considered her empty mug. "No. I don't think so. You want to know why I married Lawrence?"

"Why?" Carter asked curiously.

"Because I was never going to love him like I loved Harry." Aliana blinked back tears. "Because he was the wrong choice. I almost hated him even when I liked him. I don't know, that would have made sense a couple of beers ago. I just mean…"

Her voice trailed off, and she lifted a shoulder.

"You did what you had to do," Carter assured her, "to get through it. And we're here now to help you clean up after it and get you back to wherever you want to be."

Aliana smiled at him. "You don't have to do that."

"We're family, Ali." He shrugged. "Just try to stop us, huh?"

Aliana wiped her eyes. "Someone cutting onions in here or what?"

"I won't tell anyone you got sniffly, don't worry." He laughed and looped an arm around her shoulders. "Honestly, if you wanted to come live here... Maybe? No? Well, keep it in the back of your head. And for now, I got you a present."

"A present? Is it five more sandwiches, maybe?"

"Good grief, child. No. It's—well, you know how you asked about the mine?"

"Yeah." Aliana let her feet thud to the floor. She'd managed to forget all about Zinqued, who was back at the *Palpari*, but now she remembered everything and the beer was making her feel pleasantly invincible. "Tell me everything. How'd you hear about it?"

"I was *there* for some of it," Carter said conspiratorially. "Elisa, too. She blew up a Shrillexian."

Aliana choked on a mouthful of sandwich. *"What?"*

"My hand to God." He grinned at her. "Anyway, I wasn't there for all of it, so...I got you the guy who *was*."

"Oh?" Aliana saw him looking over her shoulder and turned around as she took another bite of sandwich.

She realized too late who Carter must mean, and she had just come up with the idea to go upstairs and climb out a window when it became clear she was out of time on that front. A man with reddish-brown hair sat down across the table from her easily. He was smiling, and his blue eyes were very warm. He was dressed somewhat anachronistically in gray slacks and a vest over a button-down shirt, but it suited him.

"Aliana," Carter said, cheerfully unaware of the fact that he'd just unleashed Aliana's worst nightmare, "meet Barnabas."

CHAPTER FOURTEEN

Absolute panic—that was what flashed through Aliana's head when Carter introduced her. She stared at Barnabas like a deer in the headlights, and Barnabas was treated to a full run-down of her thoughts, which included—

Shinigami.

Yes?

You will not believe who Carter's niece works for.

Who? Wait! I can guess.

Oh, I don't think you can. Barnabas fought the urge to laugh as he watched Aliana plaster a smile on her face. She was trying to be nonchalant, but she wasn't even close to succeeding. She looked like a cross between a gargoyle and a guilty child.

Holy fucking shitballs, she's not one of the Yennai people, is she?

No, definitely not. Dial it back a bit.

Uh...I'm trying to predict human behavior, which is already a shitshow, and it's a prediction for someone I've never met. I give up.

Zinqued—you know, the one who keeps trying to steal the ship?

You have got to be fucking kidding *me.*

Nope. Barnabas took a sip of his juice and enjoyed the frantic wash of Aliana's thoughts. *They brought her in to learn about me and con us, and she was really not expecting Carter to know me. Speaking of whom...*

He looked at Carter, who—unaware of the background conversation—had launched into a delighted introduction, highlighting both Aliana's and Barnabas' respective careers. A quick peek into his mind showed that Carter had absolutely no idea what Aliana was up to. He was simply happy that someone named Lawrence hadn't shown up, and he was sure that his niece was on a good path.

Barnabas wasn't going to correct him. After all, it made sense to learn more about Aliana's plan before she found out he could read her thoughts. Also, it was going to be funny as hell to mess with her. Barnabas was planning to ask a *lot* of detailed questions about her current job.

"—she's had a bad couple of years," Carter was saying, "but she's doing better now and—Aliana, what *are* you doing now? I just realized I don't know."

"Yes," Barnabas said wickedly. "What do you do, Aliana?"

Aliana's thoughts showed that she was seriously considering throwing her sandwich as a distraction and booking it out of the bar. "I, uh…" She gave the two of them a look. "Well, you know how it is. When you need work, you take whatever you can."

Barnabas affixed a pleasantly curious expression on his face, took a sip of juice, and let the silence grow.

"So I'm, uh…" Aliana fixed her gaze on the ceiling and said an internal prayer to get through this discussion without Barnabas figuring out what she did. "I'm on a little cargo ship," she said with a shrug. "Kind of embarrassing compared to everyone else here."

Barnabas would have been manifestly unimpressed with this attempt at redirection if he had not sensed that she was being honest. He saw in a flash a man with bristle-short brown hair smiling at Aliana, and a beautiful planet out the window of a spacecraft behind him. There was a sense of purpose in the memory, and a deep, wrenching feeling of loss.

Aliana *was* embarrassed at what she'd come to, and Barnabas was getting ready to look through her memories when he pulled his mind back, feeling as if he had over-stepped. Things related to the *Shinigami* were his business.

Things related to Aliana's life before that were not.

So he shrugged. "I was a monk for many years, and before that… Well, let us say my life was by and large a meaningless blur and I would rather forget most of it." Particularly his conversion into one of the Nacht. *That* memory still made him shudder. "A temporary posting on a cargo ship is hardly embarrassing."

Aliana took another bite of her sandwich to avoid having to answer, and Barnabas felt his lips twitch. She was clever, he'd give her that.

"Yeah, Ali," Carter added. "You know I ran around on cargo ships for *years*."

"Right," Aliana said. "Look, it's not important, okay?"

"Right," Carter agreed, clearly sensing the tension in the air but not knowing quite what to attribute it to. "Well, anyway, you wanted to know the story of the mines. Barnabas can tell you all of it."

Barnabas knew that Aliana now wanted nothing more than to run away and hide, but she lifted her chin and directed a very pleasant smile at him. "Of course," she said, and her tone was warm and engaged. "Thank you for coming to speak to me." She looked at Carter. "Thank you for calling him."

There was affection when she looked at him—a sense of safety, and the acknowledgment that Carter had tried to do something nice for her. Barnabas sensed that Aliana wouldn't do anything to make her uncle look bad, so she was determined to find a way through this as politely as possible.

Despite himself, he liked that.

"Well, then," he said. "The Etheric Empire was being dissolved, and I had left my posting as an Empress' Ranger."

"You were Ranger One." She gave him a look that said she knew she wasn't going to find a way to steal his ship, but the acceptance was tinged with wry humor instead of bitterness.

"Yes," Barnabas replied, "I was. Has Carter introduced you to Ranger Two yet?"

"He knows more of you?" Aliana gave her uncle a despairing look, but she seemed to have decided that this whole thing was funny more than anything else.

"Tabitha is very nice," Carter interjected. With a touch of pride, he added, "She loves the sandwiches here."

"They're very good," Aliana said, smiling as she patted his arm. She was happy to see that he enjoyed his work; that much was clear. She looked back at Barnabas a moment later. "I'm sorry. You were saying?" There was determination behind that smile. She had decided she was going to get through this.

"Mm, yes." He took another sip of juice. "It was mostly chance, honestly." He ignored Carter's snort. "I came to Tethra, decided to stop for a drink in this very bar, and met the Ubuara who owned it at the time, Aebura. She told me about her time in a nearby mine, and the fact that her fellow workers never seemed to have made it out—even though the mines had officially been shuttered." He gave a bland smile. "So I helped shut it down."

Carter gave another snort and rolled his eyes.

"He single-handedly led an assault on the mine, turned the vice-overseer over to his side, converted their *guard force*, and then went after the parent company that owned all of it." His voice was animated. "He's not even telling you any of the good parts!"

"I figured if Aliana had any specific questions she would ask." Barnabas smiled at the young woman. "Do you?"

His tone had apparently grown a little too smooth because she gave him a curious look. He could tell from both her thoughts and her expression that she wondered if he was onto her.

Damn. Barnabas backtracked hastily. "It's simply that I don't know what parts you already knew. I wouldn't want to take up all of your time on Tethra."

"He thinks he's bragging," Carter said. "Which he's not, since you asked."

Barnabas hid his smile. Carter, even though he had the situation all wrong, did realize that this all felt uncomfortably like bragging. Moreover, Carter's thoughts said clearly that he was quite grateful for Barnabas' intervention at the mine. Although Carter had only met most of the mine workers after they were freed, many of them had become close friends.

"It can be difficult to talk about oneself," Aliana said with surprising severity. She reminded Barnabas of nothing so much as a young lady's governess. "Don't give him a hard time."

"I'm interested where you heard the story," Barnabas stated casually. He was amused at the spike of worry he felt in Aliana's thoughts. "It shouldn't be well-known off of High Tortuga. It's not even very well-known *on* High Tortuga."

It was amusing to watch Aliana's mind race through different options, discarding some as too improbable, others as too risky.

"I met another human on Border Station 7," she said finally with a shrug. "They mentioned that they'd worked with some former miners, aliens who'd been imprisoned on High Tortuga. They said some of the mine owners had tried to hold out and not obey the Empress' orders. I was interested in the story." She saw a gap in her lies and filled it hastily. "And since I didn't have anywhere to be just yet, when Uncle Carter asked me to come visit, I did." She smiled at Carter. "It's been too long since we caught up. I didn't even know he had kids."

"How *are* the twins?" Barnabas asked Carter. "And Elisa? And the little one, of course."

"There's *another* kid?" Aliana demanded.

"Not just yet," Carter said. "Elisa's pregnant. The twins…" He sighed. "Alanna wants to be a vigilante when she grows up just like her Uncle Barnabas, so Elisa might not be best pleased with you. Although she *may* just think a vigilante is someone who shows up periodically with presents, so…"

Barnabas laughed.

"Alanna?" Aliana asked.

"I know. I asked if she'd consider Aliana instead, but apparently it's one of her favorite characters from a book, so there was no budging on that one." He grinned at his niece. "And Samuel is the other one."

"Alanna and Samuel. I like it. Any names for the next one—or is it twins again?"

From the look on Carter's face, he hadn't considered that possibility. "Oh, no."

"I-I didn't mean… Oh, dear." Aliana shot Barnabas a look of appeal. *Help!*

She didn't know he could hear her thoughts, of course, but the expression was clear enough. He gave her a tiny nod and reached over to pat Carter's hand.

"Twins are very rare," he comforted the other man. "And even if it *is* twins—"

Carter gave a strangled noise of despair.

"Even if it *is* twins," Barnabas continued serenely, "you'll have all the babysitters you could ever need."

"I'll come to stay," Aliana offered. "Give you and Elisa a hand. And, uh, I'm sure Barnabas will…" She trailed off. "Sorry," she mouthed at him.

He gave her a "Don't worry about it" headshake. "We'll

be back to help at the bar, and Tafa is probably a good babysitter. I get that vibe."

"You just want to run the bar so you can steal all the juice." Carter stabbed a finger at Barnabas in a mock accusation. He'd recovered his equilibrium, though, and was smiling again. "I know we'll get through it just fine if there are two, but it was *not* easy last time, let me tell you."

"I'm sure," Barnabas agreed with feeling. He'd seen several children grow up on the *Meredith Reynolds,* and had never figured out how the parents he knew didn't go completely insane. "Now, Aliana—"

Problem, Shinigami reported.

What's wrong? Don't tell me Zinqued made his move while Aliana was here?

I would refer to that *as a "show," not a problem.* He could feel her amusement radiating through the Etheric, but she sobered quickly. *No, it's...you have a message. You should come back and see this.*

Shinigami, what is it? Barnabas swallowed.

She hesitated, and he knew she was weighing whether to tell him—and that was what told him how serious it was.

It's Jeltor, she said finally. *Admiral Jeqwar says she has good reason to believe he's been killed.*

CHAPTER FIFTEEN

Barnabas didn't remember exactly how he got back to the ship. He'd been around long enough to excuse himself politely without giving the process any conscious thought. He had a vague impression of both Carter and Aliana looking worried, but he was gone a moment later, running through the streets of Tethra and not caring who saw him moving at unusual speeds.

He thought he saw Zinqued hanging back in an alleyway with Tik'ta, but he did not give them any attention, and they made no move toward him. That was a good choice on their part. Barnabas was *not* in a forgiving mood right now.

He came in the door of the ship at a dead sprint and made his way to the conference room, adjusting his shirt and vest with sharp, angry gestures. Shinigami was waiting there with Gar and Tafa, all of them looking somber.

Barnabas did not meet their eyes. He could not trust his composure if he did. He only nodded brusquely in Shinigami's direction and took a seat. He would behave as if he had the wherewithal to sit still, and hopefully, the act would become a reality.

Admiral Jeqwar appeared on the screen. Her body was very still in its tank, and the biosuit's voice was flat and expressionless.

"Hello," she said. "You are receiving this message because you have been deemed trustworthy by the Admiralty Board of the Jotun Navy. We continue our fight to make our government once more serve the Jotun people."

Barnabas waited, drumming his fingers on the desk anxiously. He realized that Admiral Jeqwar must at all times speak as if her messages would be found and disseminated, but he only wanted to know one thing: what she knew about Jeltor.

"I have grave news," Jeqwar continued. "After bringing the Admiralty Board news of great importance, Captain Jeltor was sent on a solo mission to uncover information about a false committee that has been deceiving the Senate as to its true purpose."

"She's good," Shinigami murmured. She was leaning against the wall, arms crossed. Her eyes didn't waver from the video. "She gets to claim that she never went against the *Senate*, just traitors whom they should also condemn."

Gar and Tafa nodded. Barnabas swallowed and kept watching.

"Unfortunately," the admiral said, "immediately after leaving the briefing, Captain Jeltor was attacked and captured."

A video appeared on screen: security footage slowed down to show Jeltor walking awkwardly through the streets—or at least, a Jotun in a biosuit. Something was off, however.

"That's not his suit," Barnabas said to Shinigami.

"She sent details about that," Shinigami replied. "They met in disguise. That *is* him."

Barnabas settled back in his chair, frowning. *What if it's her?* he asked Shinigami. They watched as Jeltor was apprehended by two other Jotuns. Jeltor was incapacitated immediately. His biosuit froze and was picked up by a gravitic device of some sort before being rotated and placed in the back of a vehicle. The whole operation took only a few seconds; they had planned this.

We can check, Shinigami said, *but from everything I've seen of her, she's the real deal. She was in this the same way Jeltor was —she didn't want it to be happening, but she was going to do her duty.*

Keep checking in on her when you can, but if you're not worried, we'll let that go for now.

They watched another loop before Admiral Jeqwar reappeared onscreen. "The two Jotuns who apprehended Captain Jeltor are known assassins. After analysis of the holo, it appears that Captain Jeltor was killed instantly. Please report any communication that purports to be from Jeltor or anyone who has disguised themselves as the captain and tries to make contact with you."

The video cut off.

"Oh," Shinigami said. She looked at Barnabas. "I see."

Barnabas gave her a nod.

"What?" Gar looked between them. "What do you see?"

"She doesn't think he's dead," Barnabas said. "She thinks he's been taken to be mind-wiped."

"*What?*" Tafa sounded horrified. "Jeltor? I know that they can mind-wipe people, but they took *him?*"

"It makes sense," Gar admitted. Now that he'd followed Barnabas' and Shinigami's leap, he could see the logic. "Who would they all trust more than anyone? Jeltor is the main figure in all this. They're the ones who run the fleet—the admirals, I mean—but Jeltor was there from the start, finding out all of what they'd done with the Yennai Corporation and exposing it. He was probably the best person the committee could have chosen."

Barnabas had to agree.

"But then why say…" Tafa's voice trailed off. She looked at her lap, and when she looked up again, she was furious. "They don't think he can be saved," she said angrily. "They want people to behave like he's just…gone. Like he's never coming back."

Barnabas nodded quietly. "Yes, they do."

"It's not right!"

Once, Barnabas knew, Tafa and Jeltor had not liked each other very much. They had been taken hostage by the same mercenary group and had been forced to rely on each other to survive. Once they had been rescued by the crew of the *Shinigami*, however, they had developed a true friendship.

He looked at her gravely. "I don't think it's right, either. Jeltor is our friend, and we won't rest until he's safe. With that said, I understand why she did what she did. If Jeltor is in their hands, he might very well have been mind-wiped already, and if he has been, he truly *is* an enemy. They cannot afford to be moved by pity, Tafa."

"Couldn't she just say something like he's dangerous

and don't tell him anything? To capture him instead of killing him?"

"They could try. What if he hijacked whatever ship he was aboard? He has a security clearance, and he knows how ships work, so he could easily do damage to the fleet and access information that would help the committee. Tafa, he's *dangerous*." He saw her angry retort coming and held up a hand. "I promise we will do everything in our power to save him. I think we have a good chance. For all we know, he hasn't even been wiped yet—and even if he has, we'll find a way to undo it. But we need to be careful."

Her two-thumbed hands clenched, but at last, she nodded and looked away.

"So let's talk about that," Barnabas said. "Right now. Because we can't delay for a moment. If the Navy finds Jeltor first he's in danger, so we need to find out where they took him to be wiped and learn anything we can about that process so that we can undo it if necessary."

Everyone nodded.

"Who knows where he is?" Barnabas asked. "Think. Members of the committee—maybe. Probably, some do, and some do not. Some staff or aides."

"The assassin might know," Gar suggested.

"*I* might know," Shinigami pointed out.

Everyone looked at her.

"I got a ton of data," she said. "The problem is, no one keeps nice little lists of where all the secret bases are with coordinates or anything. They just mention 'the research station' or whatever. But with the digging I can do otherwise, maybe there's enough of a clue."

"Good," Barnabas stated firmly. "Work on that and tell

us what you find. Next step: we need to move Jeltor's family somewhere he can't find them."

Gar's mouth dropped open in horror. "I hadn't thought of that."

Barnabas only nodded grimly. He wished that he hadn't thought of it either, but after some of the missions he'd seen, he knew to secure civilians away from trouble if at all possible. In this case, Jeltor had to be assumed to be an enemy.

He wasn't looking forward to explaining that to Jeltor's wife. What would it be like, he wondered, to know that your spouse of many years still lived but was wholly unreachable?

He promised himself and her—and Jeltor—that he would find a solution.

"We should also send a message to Admiral Jeqwar," Barnabas continued slowly. His mind was churning. What should the message say? How could he keep the true meaning of the words hidden while convincing her to help them save Jeltor's life? Should he even admit to her what his plan was?

Shinigami was having the same thoughts, and she looked at him calmly. "I recommend simply telling her you received the message," she advised. "That way, she's not worried about you not knowing what to do if you see him, and you don't have to argue with her about undoing the mind-wipe."

Barnabas nodded. "I'll compose—"

"No need. I can do it." She seemed to have forgotten her body as she handled ship functions, research, and sending a message all at once, but finally, she said, "I have four potential locations for the research facility."

"That was quick," Barnabas exclaimed, surprised.

She gave him a withering look. "I'm an AI, remember? What would take you weeks takes me seconds."

"Yes, yes." Barnabas waved her over to the table. "We're all insufferably stupid, and it's very trying. You're a saint in the body of a robot. Now come tell us what you found."

"I wouldn't say 'insufferably stupid,'" she argued, coming over to sit. "Sometimes you're quite clever. It helps that you make strange mental leaps without any logic."

"Shinigami…"

"Ah, right." Shinigami brought a map up on one of the screens. "All right. The closest location to us now would be Herothe, owned by an interspecies-conglomerate that rents to any number of companies. Aliens there—including alien captives, depressingly—probably wouldn't attract any attention."

Barnabas nodded.

"Next up, we have Klefk'ong, a Hieto world that has several locations leased to a corporation the committee runs. Or owns. Or is somehow involved with."

"Maybe Zinqued could help us with that," Barnabas suggested blandly.

Shinigami snorted. "Ask Carter's niece and see what she says. Third, we have Gokrun III, which you'll all remember as the place we nearly drowned while fighting a robot army. A lovely memory, and perhaps worth revisiting."

"Speak for yourself," Gar muttered. "One of those things gave me a bruise I can *still* feel."

"Given the upgrades we gave you in the Pod-doc that's physiologically impossible," Shinigami informed him.

"I think he was making a joke," Barnabas told her.

"Oh. Heh." She returned to her presentation. "And last but not least, Jotuna D is the fourth moon of Jotuna, and it has some sort of secret base *thing* on it."

"Is there a good path between them all?" Barnabas asked.

"Not so much, but given how fast I can travel…" She gave a self-satisfied little shrug.

Barnabas grinned. "I'm going to use your self-confidence as a barometer to tell whether *you've* been mind-wiped. If you're insufferably pretentious, we can assume it's you."

"Careful, smart guy." She gave him a smirk. "I don't think you want to turn this into a list of everyone's personality flaws."

"Yes," Tafa said severely. "Both of you, stop it. And I say we go to Gokrun III first."

"Why?" Barnabas asked, his focus instantly shifting back to the matter of Jeltor.

"Because…" Tafa paused, apparently not having gotten all of her thoughts in order. "Right. First of all, I think they're doing it on a planet they own. The Jotuns like to think they're better than everyone else, and people like that want to flaunt it, but the committee has been very good about keeping things quiet. They'll do it on a Jotun planet. That's my guess, anyway."

"All right," Barnabas said. "And as to Jotuna D…"

"Too close to the planet," Tafa shot back with a shrug.

"It's not a strong reason, I know, but anything that close is going to attract more traffic and suspicion, right?"

"Easier for senators to sneak away, though," Gar said.

"*That* might attract attention in and of itself," Shinigami pointed out. "I say we stop at Gokrun III first and then head on to the moon if we don't find anything?"

"Then it's settled," Barnabas said. "We should leave immediately, although…"

"Although?" Shinigami prompted after a moment.

"I have an idea," Barnabas said with a slightly evil grin. "One moment."

He brought up his computer and typed a message to Carter:

Carter,

I'm sorry for my unexpected departure. I hope I can make it up to you and Aliana. I'll be back in Tethra soon (a week, maybe) to have some repairs done on the Shinigami, *and hope Aliana will be there so we can have a longer discussion.*

Barnabas

"We're having repairs done?" Shinigami asked. "In *Tethra?*"

"Of course not," Barnabas said, "but they're going to think the ship will be grounded and vulnerable, not to *mention* they'll think they can put on blue coveralls and just sneak inside. It'll keep them all there while we track down the committee. If nothing else," he added, "it should save their lives. Remember when they ended up directly between us and the Yennai missiles?"

"That's a much better reason to bring them along," Gar pointed out. "That saved our asses."

"Good point, but we're going to leave them here for now. Shinigami, are we underway?"

"Yes." Shinigami stood up and stretched, an affectation she had seemingly picked up from Carter. "Anyone up for a round of sparring?"

CHAPTER SIXTEEN

As he had instructed it to do, Feword's biosuit woke him in the middle of the night. A trickle of chemicals gradually brought him out of his sleep cycle and then pumped him up with a carefully mixed cocktail that would give him the energy of an adrenaline rush, but no shaking or nerves.

The suits of all the committee members and guards had similar mechanisms built in, meant to allow them to operate without error at unusual times. Rather than trusting the whims of a good night's sleep, they could be alert and awake whenever the situation required it.

In this case, while the rest of the research facility was asleep.

Feword activated his suit controls and began to make his way carefully through the halls. He had been very thorough in his patrols over the last week, and he had reviewed many hours of security footage from the labs. He needed to make sure that he understood every automated security system that was in place.

So far, the scientists seemed to have been sincere when they'd said that they did not waste their time thinking about potential attacks. They did not seem to do even the most basic scans when they entered rooms, they did not make a point of checking the security feeds each day, and their logons to the computers were very simple. When they left the laboratories at night, they did not activate any motion sensors or other alarms.

Feword would need to speak to Grisor about this at the earliest opportunity. He was here for now, and that would be good enough, but whoever had designed the security protocols should be fired—or executed. They couldn't allow anyone who knew about the facility to survive, after all.

And in the meantime, Feword would build new protocols and teach the scientists to use them.

But that was not the purpose of tonight's excursion. Feword took the stairs down from the sleeping quarters, making sure to use the set on the far side of the building. The echoes of his steps could be more easily controlled than the sound of the elevators activating.

He did not want the scientists to wake up.

He had known for several days now that he would have to do this. Almost immediately after arrival, he had realized that the facility was short-staffed, and he knew that was not a mistake the committee would have made. They had deep pockets and did not hesitate to spend money in pursuit of their goals.

Which meant that part of the research team was missing.

Feword had not bothered Grisor with this news. Grisor trusted him implicitly to resolve issues, and Feword did not intend to tell him anything until the mystery was solved and fixed. He had his suspicions, in any case. The scientists had been so casual when they spoke of what would happen if someone broke in to attack them.

That must be because they had already survived an attack, Feword reasoned. And if they were not mentioning it to the guards, if they had hidden it from Grisor...well, what explained that?

A partial mutiny. They feared that they would be held responsible for their fellow scientists' missteps.

Feword knew they did not have to worry about this, especially if they had fended off the attack. Grisor made a point of not killing underlings for circumstances outside their control. However, things were going well enough that he did not want to cause any more chaos with what would inevitably turn into an investigation, followed by an influx of new scientists.

No. They were close with Jeltor. They did not have any time to spare. Feword would help, and when this crucial phase was over, he would tell Grisor what had happened.

He gave a pleased ripple as his biosuit opened the door to the laboratory and turned on the lights. Feword thrived on action, not on the endless talking and planning that others seemed to enjoy. He had watched the scientists over the past few days, and even that phase of watching and waiting had tested his patience.

Now he was ready to act. He looked at the central tank

in satisfaction. Jeltor was sleeping, his body scarred from the chemicals in his tank and limp with exhaustion.

Feword went to the tank's controls and brought up the chemical and tape history. The scientists had given a demonstration for Grisor, but they had since been more gentle with Jeltor. They were apparently worried that the male would break, leaving only a husk.

They were running out of time. It would be no use to convert Jeltor once the Navy realized what had happened. Feword gave a decisive nod, queued up the successive waves of chemicals and the tapes of Grisor's voice, and activated the machine.

In the tank, Jeltor's body jerked. He thrashed in desperation and fluttered to one side of the tank, pressing against the glass. It was an instinctive act, and when it gave him no relief, he began to fling himself around the tank. Feword could see from the motions of his tentacles that Jeltor was begging for an end to the pain, but the audio output of the tank had been turned off.

Feword shook his head slightly. The scientists were dedicated to their work, that much was indisputable—they never seemed to take breaks—but they were, like many civilians, emotionally weak. They did not want to listen to Jeltor's pleading.

That pleading, however, provided a clue as to Jeltor's mental state, which Feword must know in order to convert him.

When he was done here tonight, he would erase any trace of himself from the computers and leave the laboratory exactly as he'd found it. The scientists would do their work, unaware of his intervention, and during the nights, Feword would continue to break Jeltor.

He switched on the audio, and the sound of Jeltor's pleading echoed through the laboratory.

"No! *Stop!* Please, stop it—make it stop, make it stop, make it stop—hurts—please—"

Feword could see why the scientists had found this distasteful, but it had to be done. He linked his hands behind his back and began to pace, sighing as he did so. His job was not always pleasant, but he always had—and always *would*— do what he must do to help the committee.

Like many others, Feword had found the committee through service to one of its members. When his first employer had been driven out of the Senate, Feword had taken his recommendation to work for Grisor. He was assured that Grisor was devoted to the cause of Jotun supremacy in the sector.

At first, Feword had doubted this. Grisor did not make fiery speeches in the Senate, and he did not have as many enemies. How devoted could he be, if he was not publicly devoted to the cause?

Over time Feword had come to appreciate Grisor's methods, however. Grisor didn't pick fights that he knew would lead nowhere. He did not waste his time with speeches that would not convince his opponents. Feword did not want to admit it, but Grisor made his former employer look foolish—a firebrand with spirit, but no strategy.

And Grisor, once he had realized that Feword was capable and discreet, had promoted Feword to working for the committee. There he had found his true calling: doing his part to spread the rule of the Jotuns across the sector, and someday, beyond. The Jotuns were stronger and more intelligent than any other species, transcending their physical limitations with better technology than anyone else had.

Of course, the Etheric Empire had seemed like it might become a problem...but they were a Federation now and were apparently not interested in aggressive expansion. The Jotuns would easily triumph against them, Feword was sure of it.

In the tank, Jeltor's pleading had begun to break down, and he was starting to echo the words on the tape. This seemed like a good sign to Feword. He returned to the controls, considered for a moment, and increased the intensity of the chemicals.

He could not keep from rippling in happiness. Soon he would be able to contact Grisor and tell him that the conversion was complete. They would send Jeltor back into the nest of vipers that was the Admiralty Board, and Jeltor would begin to take the Navy down from the inside.

Feword felt nothing but contempt for the admirals. They were the best and brightest the Jotuns had to offer, and instead of using their talents to further the cause, they were attempting to uncover the committee and destroy it. Feword could not understand their behavior.

He did not have to understand it, he told himself. He only had to stop them.

And Jeltor was the key.

CHAPTER SEVENTEEN

C arter finished reading Barnabas' message and smiled. Barnabas could certainly be scary if someone offended his sensibilities, but those same sensibilities meant he was also very courteous and kind. In this case, he was going to come back shortly for maintenance Carter *knew* he didn't need, just to make sure Aliana hadn't been offended by him rushing off.

Carter would have written back and said that Barnabas didn't need to worry if he thought it would do any good. He knew it wouldn't, though. Once Barnabas had decided he needed to do something, he didn't let anything stand in his way.

Outside, shrieks sounded in the afternoon air. Aliana had given Carter and Elisa a break with childcare and was presently playing a game with the twins that seemed to be a cross between hide-and-go-seek, tag, and Aliana-is-a-jungle-gym. The three of them had promised not to bump into any of the fruit trees that were growing behind the bar, but everything else seemed to be fair game. Chairs had been tipped over, a table was being used as a barricade, and toys littered the ground.

The kids were occupied, and Aliana was having a good time; those were the two things that counted. Carter had seen her unwind considerably since she'd gotten here, and he was hoping he could persuade her to quit her job and stay on High Tortuga. Cargo ship workers were a dime a dozen. Her boss wouldn't have any trouble replacing her, and it was hardly going to be difficult for her to get a better job—even if she *didn't* want to work at the bar.

Carter headed down the stairs with a smile on his face and came out in time to watch Aliana flop dramatically to the ground and pretend to be dead while the twins clambered all over her, giving what Carter assumed were victory yells.

"I see you're winning," he remarked.

"Daddy!" The twins leapt up and came at him in a rush.

Aliana propped herself up on her elbows and laughed as Carter pretended to fend off the attack. "A foolish mistake, Grasshopper. They cannot be defeated."

Carter grinned and allowed himself to be pulled to the ground and turned into a new jungle gym. "So, I heard from Barnabas."

Aliana had gotten up slowly, and now she kept her back to him for a long moment while she dusted off her clothes. When she turned around, her expression was polite and detached. "Oh?"

Carter frowned at her. "Something wrong?"

"No, of course not." She gave him a smile and a shrug

and came to help Samuel get up when he tumbled onto the grass.

Carter kept frowning, but she didn't look up. "Should I not have asked him to come?"

Aliana looked up, suddenly worried. "Oh, no! No. It was really very nice of you."

"It just seemed like maybe you weren't so happy to meet him." Carter sighed. "I mean…was it too much? I know it seems like he's some big deal, but that's not how he acts. I thought…well, I thought you'd like to meet him, that's all. I remember how excited you were to help, all those places you found yourself."

Aliana sat down. Her eyes were squeezed shut, and Carter could tell she was trying not to cry.

"I'm sorry," he said automatically.

She shook her head. "It's okay," she said when she found her voice. "You did a really good thing to call him. I'm glad you have him and his friends to…well, watch over you."

"And be *friends*," Carter stated meaningfully.

She frowned at him in confusion.

"Ali, do you have *any* friends right now?"

"Of course I have friends." She looked insulted. She crossed her arms—and then realized he was waiting for her to name them. "Oh, come on. I have… Well, there's—" She sighed and rubbed her hair. "Don't look at me like that! I mean, there's Katie."

"How long has it been since you saw Katie? Okay, since you *spoke* to Katie. In any form."

She sighed. "Years."

"Yeah, see, that's my point!"

"What, that I'm lame and have no friends? Thanks."

"That you could maybe…stand to…" Over the years, Carter had learned the signs that he was on dangerous ground, and when Aliana crossed her arms and looked at him, he knew this was one of those times. "Look, you're on some random job because it was all you could get, and I *get* that, Ali, I do. But we're *here,* and we could give you a place to crash while you looked for something better. And there are a lot of people you could actually be friends with here, not just random coworkers who might or might not be low-level criminals on the run, you know?"

She harrumphed. "Everyone on my present crew is… Okay, I see your point. I just don't want to take charity, Uncle Carter. I really don't."

"I know how that feels, but I think you established that by not calling us when Lawrence took your ship. You're here now. Let us help you. Please?"

"I want to get back at him," she shot back.

"I know," Carter replied soothingly. "And you can. With a better job here, you'll be able to do that, right?"

Privately, he hoped that Aliana would get a good job here, make some friends, put down some roots, and forget about Lawrence. But even if she didn't, he had made a good point about this being the best way to go about it.

She frowned at him. "Look," she said finally. "I can't just leave them in the lurch. Let me check if they need me for this run, and then we can go from there."

Carter chewed his lip. He knew if he let Aliana go off on another trip, the odds were pretty high that she wouldn't come back to High Tortuga afterward.

So, with a silent apology to Elisa and to any deities who might care that he was lying, he pulled out the big guns.

"Hey, Samuel, Alanna—you want some cake?"

Delighted shrieks assaulted his ears.

"Cool—. I think I saw Qaladra making one. Why don't you go see?" They ran inside as quick as their tiny legs could carry them, and he took a deep breath and committed to the lie.

He went to sit next to Aliana. "Look, I wasn't entirely honest when I said I wanted you to come so I could tell you about the mine."

"What do you mean?" Aliana looked at him, worried.

"You haven't spent much time with Elisa yet," Carter explained, "so maybe this just seems crazy to you, but I swear—this pregnancy is *really* hard on her."

"Oh." Aliana swallowed. "I had no idea. She seems so happy all the time."

"She's a rock star," Carter agreed. "She'd never in a million years admit that she's having trouble, but I can see it, and I guess I thought... Well, when you wrote, it just seemed like the universe lining up, you know? I thought, 'Aliana and Elisa would get along so well.' You're great with the kids, and Elisa really likes you." It helped that a good portion of this monologue was true because Carter wasn't great at lying. "So I hoped that if you came here and saw the bar and everything, maybe you'd want to stay."

He looked at her. "I miss you. You're seriously one of my favorite people in the family. Everyone else wanted to be homebodies, but I really felt like you *got* it, you know? Traveling all over, seeing new sights. I'd love to have you work at the bar. There are so many new people coming through Tethra every day, you'd never get bored..."

"I had no idea," Aliana repeated. She rubbed her forehead. "Why didn't you just *ask*?"

Because this is all a lie I made up on the spur of the moment? Carter plastered a smile on his face and shrugged. "I didn't know how to. And, well, Elisa would *kill* me if she knew I was saying all this."

That part was *definitely* true.

"Uncle Carter." Aliana reached over to squeeze his hand. "Of *course*, I'll stay if you need help. As long as you need me." She smiled at him reassuringly. "And everything's going to be just fine with the pregnancy, I promise. Uh…has she seen a doctor?"

"Oh, yeah, they say everything is fine." Carter, having been backed into a corner, scrambled to come up with a new lie. "It's just, uh…you know, things can be *fine* but also really *hard*…emotionally…" Sensing that he was babbling, he shut up and smiled again, then remembered he was supposed to be sad and tried to remember how you looked when you were sad.

Aliana gave him a quizzical glance. "Well, I'm happy to stay," she said decisively. "But I *do* want to make sure my boss knows what's going on. I'm going to go talk to him, okay? That's the ship I came in on. He's still at the docks."

"You need backup?" Carter asked. He'd had his share of bosses who liked to bluster and say he owed them one thing or another.

"Oh, no, don't worry." Aliana gave him a quick hug. "I'll go talk to him and be right back, okay?"

"Sure." Happy about his victory, Carter went off to find Elisa, and located her in the basement, swearing at one of the cider presses. She'd been determined to have cider in the bar and had insisted that they make it traditionally. She seemed to be regretting her choices.

She wiped her forehead and gave him a smile and a shrug. "This cider press is possessed, I swear." Her smile faded. "What did you do?"

"What?" Carter asked innocently.

"I know that look, Eastbourne." She jabbed a finger at him. "You look guilty. You look like you did something bad. What was it? *Tell me.*"

"Okay, okay!" Carter gave a little laugh. "So, here's the story. Don't be mad…"

Aliana pushed her way through the crowd near the docks, slipping through the workers to get to the *Palpari*.

She wasn't entirely sure what she was going to say to Zinqued. The *Shinigami* was his "white whale," as Tik'ta had said, and Aliana knew that Zinqued wouldn't be happy she was giving up.

He hadn't paid her yet, though, and she was pretty sure she could scrape together enough money to pay him for the fuel it took to get here, even though he'd made a profit on their cargo run. She took a deep breath and entered the passcode on the door, yelling hello as she came into the ship.

"You're back!" Zinqued came out into the hall from the bridge. "I am so relieved. Do you know, I actually *saw* Barnabas here?"

"Ah. Right." Aliana nodded. "Yeah, I'm not surprised. Apparently, he knows people here."

"I was afraid he would recognize me!" Zinqued said. "But he did not. Lucky break, eh?"

"Yep. Lucky break." Aliana had a stroke of inspiration. "Apparently he'll be back in not too long, though, so you should probably not be here then."

"But this may be one of the best places to steal the ship," Zinqued said eagerly. "I was thinking—he almost certainly has clearance to leave at high speed without any checks, whereas on another planet, automated systems might kick in. But with this being a human planet…"

"Yes, yes. Um." Aliana sighed. "Look."

Zinqued gave her a shrewd look. "Are you quitting?"

"I…yes." Aliana swallowed. "I came here to see my uncle," she explained. "And his wife is pregnant, and she's having a really hard time, and he wants me to stay and help. I can't just turn my back on him. He's always been there for me."

"Ah." Zinqued nodded. "I understand. And I think, perhaps, you are worried that this job might be impossible, eh?"

"Okay, yes. Maybe. Given what I have heard, I don't know how to steal the *Shinigami*. Barnabas seems like someone I wouldn't want to mess with."

Zinqued, far from being annoyed, smiled broadly at her. "I know. He is a worthy competitor."

Tik'ta had come into the hallway, and she sighed at this latest pronouncement. "He's not going to pull it off," she said in a stage whisper. Her fondness for Zinqued was apparent, so Aliana smiled.

"And as no payment has been given yet," Zinqued said, looping an arm around Aliana's shoulders as she went to her cabin, "no hard feelings, eh? We made a good profit on this run to High Tortuga."

"Thanks, Zinqued." Aliana started packing, deeply relieved that he was being reasonable.

"Of course..." Zinqued gave an elegant shrug. "You won't be able to steal back *your* ship from here."

Aliana froze, a handful of socks halfway between her drawer and her duffel bag.

"What was it, the *Rayette*?" Zinqued was staring into space as though he were trying to remember. Aliana hadn't told him which ship it was, though, so he definitely knew. He'd done his research. "She's a nice ship," he said pleasantly. "And the captain, eh? Lawrence Jensen. Not a nice fellow, no. Not at all."

Aliana felt her blood pressure rising. The thought of Lawrence's smug face *always* made her want to scream. "Yep," she said, stuffing the socks in her bag and grabbing another handful. "He's a real bastard."

Zinqued nodded. "But it's nice here," he said smoothly. "A pretty town, Tethra. Very quiet. Very pleasant."

Aliana narrowed her eyes at him.

"Enough to make you forget all about your plans for revenge, I'd think," Zinqued said. He smiled at her. "I wish you luck, Aliana Eastbourne. And come find us when you want a job, eh?"

He left, and Aliana stared after him, her mind working furiously.

High Tortuga *was* a nice place. It *was* nice enough to make her forget her plans for revenge. But now that Zinqued had warned her about that, she resolved not to let this place lull her into a false sense of security.

And if Barnabas was coming back to High Tortuga...

"Wait!" She popped her head out the doorway.

Zinqued turned to look at her. "Yes?" he asked innocently.

"Just so we're clear," Aliana said, "if I could get you the *Shinigami*—if I get a shot at it—you'd still help me with the *Rayette*?"

"Why, yes." Zinqued smiled. "Yes, we would."

Aliana nodded, her mind working double-time. "All right," she said finally. "Yeah. Okay. Well, maybe you'll hear from me, then."

Like hell, she was going to let Lawrence get away with what he'd done. If the *Shinigami* was the price for that, well...she'd pay it.

CHAPTER EIGHTEEN

"So, when we arrive at the planet, we're going to do about three full orbits." Barnabas brought up a holograph of Gokrun III with a strange path traced around it. "This will allow Shinigami to scan the entirety of the planet with a low margin for error." Seeing Gar's frown of confusion, he pointed out, "The last base we saw here was underground. We need to be close enough to make sure that we notice entryways with similar construction."

Gar nodded.

"Once we know what we're dealing with," Barnabas said, "we can make a proper plan. In this case, speed is of the essence. We don't know how long Jeltor has before he's mind-wiped, so we have to go in immediately. Of course, somehow this mission requires both speed *and* stealth, which seems like a bad combination."

"Well," Tafa pointed out, "to be entirely accurate, you only need them to think they're not under attack, right? So we could try to con our way in."

"Yeah, but the Jotun we would usually use for that sort of con is the guy we're rescuing," Shinigami retorted.

"Oh." Tafa's face fell. "Right. Forgot that."

"It's a good point," Barnabas said. "And that actually gives me an idea. Shinigami, we've been talking about taking out all of their automated defense measures and their scanners and so on… What if we just tricked them?"

"Way ahead of you," Shinigami said. "We'll be doing both. When we captured the black ops ship on our last mission, I made sure to search through its communications banks. It had some protocols that I assume gave it passage through Jotun government systems, and I'll be trying those out while I take out the scanners one by one."

"Safer *is* better."

"Of course, that's assuming they aren't hardwired to set off alarms if one of them goes out of contact," Shinigami remarked contemplatively.

Everyone gave her a worried look.

"Oh, don't look at me like that, I'll figure something out." She sat back in her chair, crossing her arms, and then sat up and snapped her fingers. "Aha! I'll just learn the outgoing signal of each and teach the *Shinigami* to replicate it so that they don't notice it's gone."

"Clever," Barnabas murmured. "What is it *like* to be able to do things like that?"

"What is it like to be able to go up steps without tripping over your own feet?" Shinigami asked bitterly. "I can still only walk well if the surface is entirely flat."

"You'll get the hang of it," Barnabas assured her. The corner of his mouth was twitching.

"So I'll come out with you?" Gar asked.

"Yes. You *and* Shinigami. We need all hands on deck unless this is a very small facility, and I'm guessing it's not. If they've been studying multiple species, I'd guess there are a lot of different laboratories and…cages."

Everyone sank into silence for a moment. Gar looked like he might be sick, Shinigami looked furious, and Tafa looked—to Barnabas' surprise—just as angry as Shinigami. He had guessed that the Yofu would be scared, but she didn't look frightened.

She looked like she wanted to kill the scientists with her bare hands.

"Should I come, too?" she asked Barnabas. She was nervous but resolute. The offer was sincere. "I helped with the last mission, after all."

"You did, but, uh…" Barnabas fought his knee-jerk reaction to tell her no and considered the offer. "I have to think about that."

"Whether or not it's a good idea depends on what kinds of security they have inside," Shinigami explained. "And *that* is something we won't know until we're in there." *It's not a good idea,* she added privately to Barnabas.

It worries me too, but I don't want to reject the offer without really thinking about it.

I think faster than you, and I'm telling you it's a bad idea. She gave him a meaningful look across the room.

If she wants to get involved—

Then we see how she fares in a bar fight somewhere and go from there.

Tabitha?

Oh, good idea! We'll have her tag along with Tabitha for a bit.

No, that's not what I—goddammit. Barnabas fought the urge to laugh. To Tafa, he said, "How about this? We'll put you in some body armor that isn't obvious, and you'll wait on the ship. If the path to wherever we are going is clear and we think it's just us against the scientists, you can come along, okay?"

She considered his words, and he saw that she wanted to argue. Thankfully, however, she seemed to remember her limitations. She nodded. "I don't want to get anyone hurt. I just want to help if I can. It's *Jeltor.*"

Barnabas met her eyes and gave a nod. "I know. I feel helpless, too."

Tafa grumbled. "Yeah, but *you* get to kick the doors open and actually rescue him. What do I get to do?"

"Sneak into the Jotun Senate buildings and steal a bunch of information," Barnabas reminded her.

"Oh." She brightened considerably. "Yeah, I did do that." She nudged Gar with one elbow. "I helped," she said, very pleased with herself.

Gar grinned back at her.

I tell you, Shinigami commented, *I hope those two kids wind up together.*

They...they aren't the same species, Shinigami.

So?

Barnabas shook his head and rolled his eyes. No matter how ridiculous an idea was, once Shinigami committed to it there was no talking her out of it. He was pretty sure he could expect her to be offering little conversational hints in that direction for the next few weeks.

He sighed and brought the meeting back on track. "So, Shinigami, Gar, and I will go out immediately. Tafa will stay on the ship and get it ready for Jeltor if he needs medical assistance, and she'll join us if we need help."

Everybody nodded.

"Approaching the planet now," Shinigami reported. "And I want to remind everyone that we might not find anything."

"Let's be ready in case we do," Barnabas said firmly. "Everyone go get ready. Shinigami, tell us when you have likely candidates for landing spots."

Gil sighed as he stretched his tentacles to their fullest length and shook himself all over. He was exhausted. They had already been working every minute, skipping sleep and any breaks in order to get the experiments stabilized and the data out, and things had gotten harder when the new guards were assigned to them.

He knew it could be far worse than it was. The guards didn't suspect Gil's and Wev's true identity yet, after all. Gil had been suspicious about all of their questions, but they seemed to be genuine in their desire to help—not prying for secrets or poking into closets.

No, they thought Gil and Wev were upset about their failure to break Jeltor, and they were trying to help. It would be sweet, really...if what they were talking about wasn't destroying someone's life and bringing down multiple outside governments.

Gil shook himself. With the guards so close by, he had to stop himself from asking them why in the heavens they would support something like the committee. They seemed fully aware of the committee's goals, and Gil could not think of any reason that a Jotun would want such things.

Of course, that was not entirely true. He could understand that as the Etheric Empire shook nearby sectors, as other species rose and fell, anyone would want the safety and security of being undeniably in charge.

But he would rather throw himself in a vat of acid than trust his safety to the committee.

He came into the laboratory that housed Jeltor's tank and saw Wev bent over the controls, fingers tapping furiously.

Good morning, Gil said courteously.

There was no answer.

Wev?

Wev straightened and turned to him, and Gil knew at once that something was terribly wrong. He hurried across the room to look into the tank.

He's not responding the way he should, Wev said as Gil joined him. The two of them peered into the tank together. *I noticed that they were accessing the early morning tapes and they often liked to come by just after we started, so I'd been doing a low-acid solution in the mornings when I came in. But when I started it...*

Gil looked at the tank. Jeltor looked like he was blissfully asleep. *Are you sure the tubes are working? Are you* sure *there's acid in there?*

Very sure. Wev's voice was sharp. *You can put your tentacle in if you doubt me.*

Gil gave him a look. *No, thank you. But if he's not doing well...*

I don't understand it. Wev thrashed in frustration. *Yesterday, he was fine.*

It's possible it was simply too much for him to take, Gil stated simply. He hesitated. *It might be kinder to end it—and it would eliminate the possibility of him actually breaking.*

The two of them had discussed this before. In one sense, they were agreed—if it looked like conversion was imminent, and there was no other way to stop Jeltor from being released into the Navy like a ticking time bomb, they would kill him rather than allow him to be made a weapon.

Gil, however, had been in favor of killing Jeltor immediately and claiming it had been an accident, while Wev had argued for leniency and time. The two of them disagreed rarely enough that Gil had decided to wait.

Now, however, he was nervous enough to bring it up again.

Wev ignored the suggestion. *I don't understand,* he was muttering. *What could possibly...*

He broke off and went to a bookshelf in the corner, where binders held overflowing research notes that had been mostly-neatly organized...and then removed, scanned, and replaced by Gil and Wev. They had also brought their own cameras to monitor what went on in the lab, fearing that one of the experiments might go wrong.

Now the two of them watched the tapes from the night before—and saw Feword enter the laboratory.

No, Wev whispered. *What is he doing?*

I think it's pretty clear what he's doing.

Not that! Wev rarely yelled either, and Gil was startled into silence. Wev turned to him, looking at Gil with his actual body rather than with the biosuit's face. *If he suspected us, he would kill us. So what is this? What is he doing?*

That was a very good question, and Gil did not have the answer. He considered, pacing back to the tank that held Jeltor. They had only ever done the barest hint of the protocol on Jeltor, unsure how successful the scientists' procedure really was.

It seemed that it was very successful. In only one nights' work, Feword had nearly converted Jeltor.

We have to end it, Gil told Wev.

No! Wev was adamant.

Wev, he's a weapon, and he's almost ready to be used.

He deserves better than this. Wev stared Gil down. *Why are we even doing this if we won't help the people hurt by it?*

There were many answers Gil could give. He knew that. He could have said that letting Jeltor go free would hurt more people than it would help. He could have said that Wev had seen situations where nothing could be done, because that was true—they had been on site during numerous civilian uprisings on alien worlds, or disasters that had trapped people without any hope of them being saved.

Sometimes people *couldn't* be saved.

But Wev's tone shamed him to his core. Gil had grown cold as they had continued with this job. He had begun to make these decisions too easily.

He did not like what that said about him. He nodded to Wev and sent *something*—not words, but an impression of his mind. Wev rippled soothingly.

Do not blame yourself. Your intentions have always been good.

Gil did not trust himself to speak for a long moment. He looked at where Jeltor floated in a haze.

We have to have a plan, he said. *And it has to be today, because one more night of this and there might be nothing we can do to bring him back.*

CHAPTER NINETEEN

"Well, *here's* a problem we didn't anticipate," Shinigami announced, halfway into their second orbit of Gokrun III. She was halfway through dressing her body in armor, so she used her sensors to find Barnabas in his quarters. "I have eight potential landing sites."

"Ask Tafa to help you," Barnabas suggested. "She has a good eye for these things."

"Oh, good idea." Shinigami switched to a ship-wide channel. "Tafa, I need your help on the bridge."

"On my way!" Tafa called back. Shinigami felt her move from her quarters and into the hallways at a run.

Shinigami smiled. Now that she had a body, she could actually express emotions in an action, and she had found that she enjoyed doing so.

She continued to devote part of her attention to her armor as Tafa approached the bridge. It was blood-red, and although she had no trouble with uncomfortable or heavy armor the way a human might, she still appreciated that hers was sleek and well put together.

Barnabas was right, she decided. Wearing well-tailored clothes was something that gave you confidence in your abilities. As much as she teased him, she had to admit that he had a good sense of style—something she did *not* yet have. She had been studying her memories of Gabrielle, Ekaterina, Tabitha, and Bethany Anne, and she had no idea how she wanted to present herself. Each of them managed to look stylish in very different clothes, which was a puzzle Shinigami could make neither heads nor tails of.

On the bridge, the doors slid open for Tafa and Shinigami abandoned her musings on style. She projected a holograph of herself in the corner, already dressed in her armor, and gave an appreciative whistle at Tafa's outfit. Though Tafa did not yet have a full suit of custom armor, she looked surprisingly confident and at ease in the light-weight black bulletproof clothing she was wearing.

She smiled at Shinigami. "I am ready to help."

"Excellent." Shinigami brought up the eight potential sites, each catalogued with scans and computer-generated reconstructions. "We have more than one potential landing site, and we thought you might help us narrow it down. You tend to see details the rest of us miss."

"Oh! Of course." Tafa went to sit down and swung her head back and forth, looking at each picture out of one eye, then the other. "Hmm. I'd throw out site one. That honestly looks like the weird part of the energy signature is due to it having utility functions."

"It's in the middle of a lake," Shinigami protested. "That's suspicious."

"This is a resort planet for *Jotuns*, remember? It's probably doing something with the water and doubling as a strange hotel-thing."

"Ah, right." Shinigami made that picture disappear.

"As for the others..." Tafa examined each in turn. "I'd say five and eight are the most likely so far. Show me more on five."

"Five? Really?" Shinigami was surprised, but she wiped the other information and put up a map of energy signatures, intercepted transmissions, and a slowly-rotating 3D map of the facility.

"They're taking great care to make the output *look* like it's a manufacturing plant, but I don't buy it." Tafa shook her head. "The shape of the windows is odd. I'm actually not sure those *are* windows, and those transmissions make no sense."

"They're probably in code."

"Or they're gibberish," Tafa said. "And if you haven't cracked them already, I'm guessing that's what they are."

"Ohhhh." Shinigami studied the data with new appreciation. "Organic life forms are so sneaky. All the data here are *fake*. They mean nothing. I hate that."

Tafa smiled. "Unless you find any more, I'd say five is our best bet."

"I say we just go, and if it's not that, we try another one." Barnabas had come onto the bridge while the two of them were talking, and now he adjusted his collar slightly as he studied the screen.

"Nervous?" Shinigami asked.

"Yes," he replied flatly. "Yes, I am. Jeltor has been

missing for a week, and I have no idea how long he can hold out."

Shinigami watched him for a moment. If they went in and found the wrong facility, they risked alerting the committee to their presence *and* losing valuable time. But Barnabas wasn't stupid. He already knew what he was risking, and he didn't often allow emotion to overwhelm him.

She noted the faint dilation in his pupils and the way his pulse was beating quickly in his neck. His motions had the faint, too-quick undertone that came from adrenaline and cortisol. Yes, he was certainly experiencing strong emotions right now.

She looked at Tafa. "How sure are you that this could be the research facility?"

Tafa looked back at the screens for a long moment. "Very sure," she said, with a nod. "This facility isn't what they say it is, that's for sure, and it is the most suspicious of the lineup you gave me.

Shinigami nodded to her and Barnabas.

"Take us down, then," he said. He looked at the screens. "I'm guessing you'll have to go through that canyon directly?"

"If we don't want to go blasting in the top, yes."

The building lay at the end of a canyon with spears of rock jutting up to make landing almost impossible. The only clear way to get in was down the length of the canyon, which was narrow and filled to the brim with sensors and turrets. Landing on the roof of the facility, while it was probably possible with the *Shinigami's* maneuverability, would almost certainly alert the guards to their presence.

"What about a Pod?" Barnabas asked.

Shinigami considered this. "No good. Remember, I want to both destroy each defensive device *and* replicate its signal, and I can't do that from a Pod. If I send you down and it turns out that the signals I'm sending don't keep us invisible to their tech, we'll have a problem I can't easily solve, and the people in the facility will be alerted." She gave him a reassuring smile. "But I'll get us through that canyon quickly, I promise."

Barnabas' lips tightened, but he gave her a nod. "I know you will," was all he said, and Shinigami knew he was reassuring himself. As worried as he was, and anxious to have this over with, he wouldn't take it out on them.

Barnabas, Gar, and Tafa watched from the bridge as Shinigami descended through the atmosphere and approached the canyon. It was close to a mile long and was housed on one of the larger islands in the planet's southern hemisphere, part of a volcanic archipelago that was remarkably inhospitable to life.

"That's another thing," Tafa said. Everyone looked at her in confusion, and she smiled self-consciously. "Sorry, I was still thinking about *why* I'm so sure this is the place. If anyone escaped from that facility, it would be almost impossible to get out. The Jotun captives would have no water to swim through and the other species would have to climb straight up and out of the canyon, which is impossible, or take their chances going through the whole mile with all the turrets. Even if they'd killed everyone in the facility the automated defenses would still work, and once they got out of the *canyon*...they're in the middle of nowhere, with no edible plants or freshwater. My other top choice was in a much more hospitable place."

Everyone nodded. Given the committee's penchant for secrecy, this location made a lot of sense, and Shinigami was pleased with Tafa's analysis. It could be frustrating to watch organic life forms make huge leaps of logic, but she had learned that what they called "instinct" often produced well-founded conclusions, and they simply could not articulate the reasons yet.

She was already working to include Tafa's latest leap in her own algorithms, identifying every factor she could and trying to replicate the technique on other data.

ADAM and ArchAngel II were correct—working with organic beings was equal parts rewarding and insanely frustrating.

She moved her holograph to sit in the captain's chair as she guided the ship into the canyon. She had finished putting on her armor and decided to join the rest of the people on the bridge. Briefly, she wondered what it must be like only to do one thing at a time.

It sounded terrible.

The first part of the alert system had not seen them yet, and Shinigami created a map of every piece of machinery she could find on her scanners. A network sprang up on the screen, overlaid on the video of the canyon.

As she had guessed, each sensor fed information to the others, which allowed the sensors to move the turrets into place before any ship was even in range. Moreover, it looked as though the turrets were programmed to track any ship down the length of the canyon, whether or not it was tagged as an enemy.

That was smart, and Shinigami *hated* it when her opponents were smart. One wrong move and they'd be dealing with a veritable hailstorm of projectiles. She sighed and analyzed the first sensor's outgoing signature. Then she copied it, launched a set of pucks at the sensor, and began broadcasting its message so that there was not even a blip in the signal when it was destroyed.

Everyone on the bridge held their breath—except for Shinigami, who had no breath to hold. The doors slid open for her to walk in and she went over to the captain's chair and settled into it, melding almost perfectly with the holograph.

Her hair was always better in holograph form.

Next up was the first pair of turrets. At first, Shinigami thought they only received signals, but she realized a millionth of a second later that they also sent signals to the other turrets about their tracking speed and pinged other turrets when their target went out of range.

Because they did not seem to have noticed her yet, she was able to take them out without alerting the others. There was no data stream to interrupt.

She proceeded through the canyon carefully, destroying each sensor and set of turrets in turn and replicating all of the signals. She did not stop them as she set the ship down and began the process of preparing the airlock.

"The air is inhospitable here," she reported. "I recommend helmets for you two."

"You as well," Barnabas said immediately. "We don't want them to know what you are if they catch sight of you."

"Smart." Shinigami stood. "One other thing." She panned the camera sideways to show a Jotun ship waiting outside the building.

"There's a *ship?*" Barnabas said immediately.

"It hasn't been used in some time," Shinigami said. "Its systems are in a ready state of a sort, but it's mostly dormant. The Jotuns are *very* good with quick activation times on their technology. I'll see what I can figure out about it while we're all inside."

"Good call." Barnabas nodded to Tafa. "Stay here with the bridge *sealed,*" he instructed. He'd been careful of her feelings before, but there was no equivocation now. "Until we determine if it's safe, I don't want you to take any chances. Is that clear?"

Tafa nodded, swallowing.

"As long as you're aboard, we'll put you in charge of opening the doors," Barnabas added. "That means if anyone passes all of the automated checks somehow, they'll still have to contend with you. For verification…hmm. Just ask anyone who tries to get in for a piece of information that only the three of us would know."

"Okay." Tafa gave the Yofu version of a thumbs up: her two inner thumbs linked together, and the two outer ones pointing straight out to the sides.

Shinigami responded with the "rock on" gesture, and Barnabas snorted.

"All right," he said as the assault team left the bridge. "Let's go get our friend."

CHAPTER TWENTY

Shinigami went first as they approached the doors of the facility. That made Barnabas nervous, but she was indubitably the best one to disarm the doors and disable any alarms. She laid a palm against the door and thought for a long moment before nodding decisively. The door slid open.

Silence. No alarms. Barnabas nodded, and they crept inside.

They were in a pleasant antechamber that must be the receiving room for whatever dignitaries came to visit this place. As was the case with many Jotun spaces, water featured prominently: little streams ran along the edges of the room, providing a soothing sound and sending light bouncing off the stone walls.

It was clear that no one used this room often, however. The air carried the faint scent of a fountain that hadn't been cleaned, and the whole place had just a bit too much dust.

Barnabas and Gar kept their guard up as Shinigami scanned the room and walked the edges of it. In the end, instead of guiding them through the big doors at the center of the back wall, she went to a smaller door on one side of the room.

Which was when they heard the crying.

It was only the faintest sound, but it was enough to make Barnabas' heart twist in his chest. It wasn't in a human register, but there was no mistaking what it was: a keening wail that held no hope.

All three of them looked at each other, faces echoing the despair they were hearing. Then Shinigami turned back to her work with renewed determination and wrenched open the door to the side corridor. She strode inside without looking back, and there was no mistaking her expression.

She was ready to kill whoever was doing this with her bare hands if she had to.

Barnabas exchanged a quick glance with Gar before running after her. He caught up with her partway down the hall and was pleased to see she was slowing, drawing to one side of the corridor so she could check one of the rooms inside without being seen.

She wasn't going to let her anger get the better of her, then. That was good. She exchanged a look with Barnabas.

Do you want to do this? You're probably better at it.

Barnabas gave a quick nod and was just taking his place when the door came flying off its hinges and a Jotun was thrown out of the room to slam against the wall and slide down it.

It didn't notice them as it staggered to its feet, and a

moment later, another Jotun came running out of the room, one arm raised for a punch. The first only just made it out of the way, and the punch caught it on the arm. It leveled a strike at its attacker, but weakly.

It was clear within seconds that one of these two Jotun was trained to fight and the other was not. Barnabas held an arm out to keep Shinigami and Gar back. If one of these two was not trained in combat, they were probably the scientist—which meant the facility was under attack, and *that* meant...

He narrowed his eyes. Should they break this up?

Shinigami, if the scientists are dead, do you think you can get into their results and undo what they did?

Depends on how good they were about keeping records, Shinigami said drily. She leaned back as the stronger Jotun lifted the weaker one off its feet and slammed it into the wall.

Which was when the strong one noticed the three of them. It pulled the weaker Jotun away from the wall, slammed it into the wall once more, and turned to face them. Everything about its movements conveyed a threat, and Barnabas shifted to the balls of his feet.

"What's going on here?" Shinigami asked before anyone else could speak. Barnabas had to hand it to her; she had the command-voice *down*. She spoke like she should be answered, and to his amusement, the Jotun obeyed without thinking.

"He attacked me while I was in the records room." His mechanical voice grated; something must have gotten knocked out of place in the sound box. "I suspected that he wasn't one of the real scientists, and I was—"

That was all he got out before the water in his tank began to foam and the biosuit staggered to its knees. He'd made the mistake of taking his eyes off his opponent, and the other Jotun had managed to reach up and jam something into one of the weak points between the plates of armor.

Whatever he'd done, the stronger Jotun died quickly, and the weaker one hauled itself to its feet.

"Who are you?" it asked without preamble. And then, strangely: "Are you Barnabas?"

"I'm Shinigami," said Shinigami. She jerked her head at Barnabas. "*He's* Barnabas."

"My apologies. So the smaller humans are the females, then?"

"Mostly correct. The standard height of a male human—"

"Shinigami," Barnabas interrupted. "This is not relevant." To the Jotun, he said, "Who are *you*? That seems to be the big question."

The Jotun looked down at its opponent for a moment. "He was right. I'm not one of the scientists. I'm part of the Jotun Interplanetary Intelligence Agency, and my partner and I infiltrated this facility a month ago."

"So how did the guard not know who you were?" Gar asked.

"It's complicated," the Jotun said evasively.

"All right," Barnabas said. His tone was just a touch too pleasant, and he saw both Gar and Shinigami step back a bit so as not to be in the metaphorical line of fire. "Here's the deal: we're here to find Captain Jeltor. You seem to not be on the committee's side, so hopefully, you'll help us find him. That would be good for you. What would *not* be good for you would be to get in my way."

"You have a way to get out of here?" the Jotun asked. "Because if you can get Jeltor out, I will gladly help you do that. I'm Gil, by the way."

"Barnabas. That's Shinigami. That's Gar."

"A Luvendi wearing armor," the Jotun murmured. "Will wonders never cease!" A moment later he was back to business, however. "There are three more guards, all with suits like this one. My partner Wev is on another floor. We've been trying to isolate the guards all morning to kill them one by one. They were sent by the committee to 'assist,' us and they're close to blowing our cover. We were going to steal their ship to escape."

"Let's keep moving while we talk. But first—" Barnabas pointed. "All the records are in that room? All the data on the conversion process?"

"Yes."

"On it," Shinigami said at once. She strode into the room and groaned. "*Hard copies?*"

"The scanner in the corner will allow quick digitization of the files," Gil told them. "They were worried about someone being able to access the computer systems, so all the systems here are self-contained and the data is regularly transferred to hard copy and wiped."

"I hate competent people," Shinigami said with feeling, yanking down a file and going over to the scanner. "I hope you're okay with this room being a mess when I'm done because I'm *not* going to take the time to put everything back."

"Be my guest." Gil sounded amused. "You showing up

here is a stroke of luck, quite frankly. We knew we needed to get the data out, as well as Jeltor and as many of the experiments as we could, and we needed to kill the guards. I sense you'll all make those objectives much easier."

"That sounds correct," Barnabas said simply. He hoisted one Jean Dukes Special. "Shall we? Jeltor first."

"Ah." Gil set off, but his tone was worried. "I have...bad news about Jeltor."

"What is it?" Barnabas heard himself ask. In the records room, he heard Shinigami stop moving as she strained to hear. Gar had gone pale.

"One of the guards seems to have decided to try to hurry things along," Gil said. He led them to a junction and turned. "This way. We'll be going up two flights. You see," he said, returning to his explanation, "a week or so ago, Jeltor was delivered to us for conversion. We had spent the past few weeks before that trying to rehabilitate the other experiments, and we hadn't had much luck. We strung things out as much as we could. We weren't sure what they could see on the security feeds, so we had to *pretend* to work on Jeltor, but we weren't really doing the whole procedure. The problem is, that soldier *did* do it, and I'm afraid Jeltor is partially gone."

The elevator arrived with a little ding and Gil went to step into it, but Barnabas grabbed his arm.

"You can undo it, though, right?" His voice was dangerous.

Most people would have quailed in the face of Barnabas' anger, but Gil was not one of them. "I don't know," he said honestly. "I'm not a scientist. I sincerely hope that with this data, a way can be found to undo the damage—but I cannot be certain of that." When Barnabas said nothing, Gil continued softly, "I wish I could."

Barnabas released his arm and stepped into the elevator silently, aware of Gar's comforting presence at his side. His mind was whirling.

He only vaguely heard Gil say, "What worries me is that the conversion process creates *certainty*, and certainty is very seductive. Extremism, for instance, takes hold even when there has been no chemical conditioning like there is in this case.

"What does that mean?" Barnabas asked wearily.

"He means that to be certain of your worldview is something people desire," Gar said unexpectedly. "The world is uncertain, and people want it to not be. They'll subscribe to ridiculous beliefs just so they can feel more secure."

"Precisely," Gil said with a nod to Gar. "The Luvendi is quite correct. What makes this belief even more damaging is that it used...well, torture, to render the victim vulnerable before feeding them the information about who to obey."

Barnabas shook his head. "Those worldviews fall apart when they're tested," he said. "Not always, but they do. I'm *not* giving up on Jeltor."

"Nor should you," Gil said. "But be cautious. The process doesn't destroy function or intelligence. Jeltor is still intelligent enough to *pretend* he's been rehabilitated even if he hasn't been. You cannot allow him to be exposed to classified material. He *must* be kept secure."

"Oh, I had no intentions of letting him back into the Navy," Barnabas said.

Admiral Jeqwar shared Gil's worry, after all. She struck Barnabas as the type who preferred being safe rather than sorry.

And in this case, he was fairly sure that meant killing Jeltor and delivering a stirring eulogy at his funeral rather than taking the time to rehabilitate him.

Feword frowned at his screens. Yeldred had been on his break for far too long. Feword knew that it was distasteful work to tend the alien experiments, but that didn't mean he would allow the male to shirk his duty.

Although he *did* intend to speak to Grisor about terminating these particular experiments. They were clearly broken beyond the point of rehabilitation. The one Brakalon cried all the time, until Feword was tempted to shoot him just to get rid of the sound.

He traced Yeldred's last known location and clomped heavily down the stairs rather than using the elevator. Feword was a big believer in doing as much as he could with his suit. One should become at home enough in it that using it was like second nature.

Perhaps some combat drills might give his team more focus…

He was still thinking when he came out into the hallway, then his eyes widened.

Down the hall, was an open door, and he made his way toward it quickly, readying his weapons.

His suit was finely calibrated and able to move softly, but he hadn't ever gone up against a cybernetic body housing an Empire AI. In the records room, Shinigami had stopped moving as soon as she sensed Feword's steps in the stairwell. Near the closed door lay the guard's body, surrounded by a growing pile of scanned records. As Feword opened the door, Shinigami sank into a crouch. If he looked her way as he walked past the room, he would see nothing out of the ordinary.

He continued down the hall and toward the ship, and Shinigami flexed her hand, then clenched it, staring at the fist. She was still not as at home in her body as she needed to be to fight a trained killer.

But it looked like the time had come.

CHAPTER TWENTY-ONE

The elevator doors opened, and Gil left the elevator first. He beckoned silently once he had determined the coast was clear and Barnabas and Gar followed him, weapons at the ready.

Barnabas heard the footsteps nearby first, and a split-second later Gil motioned for them to stop. He pointed to Barnabas' gun, then pointed ahead.

Barnabas nodded and motioned to Gar to wait. He could hear that it was one Jotun, and he suspected that he could do this more quietly on his own. Silence was of the essence. No one seemed to have noticed yet that one of the guards was dead, and he wanted to keep it that way.

Barnabas, Shinigami said in his mind.

I'm a little busy right now. He paused at the corner and waited for a moment. The footsteps were going away from him, so he slipped around the corner and followed the Jotun guard as it marched along the hallway. He had to move quickly in case it decided to swivel in its tank. *What is it?*

One of the guards discovered the murdered one. He went right by the records room without properly scanning it, so he doesn't know I am there. He's going toward the main entrance.

Stay there, Barnabas said unequivocally. *I'll send Gar, and you two can take him out together.*

Roger that.

Gar—go back to the records room. Check the corridor before coming out of the stairwell. One of the guards has discovered the breach.

On my way.

Gar dropped out of contact, and with that, Barnabas leapt into action. He had never worried too much about quietness when he killed Jotuns before, so he was going to have to improvise.

He had drawn his knife, and he lunged quickly to jam it into the plating by the Jotun's knee. It tried to pivot, but without both legs it was useless. It staggered and he caught it, wary of the sound of it crashing to the ground.

Its arms were still functional and they shot out, knives and needles popping out of recessed panels. Barnabas jerked away, swore internally, and made a split-second decision. He half-stood and then came down again with all his might, breaking the tank with his fist and plunging his knife into the thrashing body.

He had no idea where any of the vital organs were, but he seemed to have hit something important because the thrashing ended and the Jotun lay still on the floor. A moment later, footsteps sounded behind him, and Barnabas looked to see Gil staring at the Jotun.

"You know," he said inconsequentially, "many believe that biosuits are completely impregnable."

"That," Barnabas said, "is not true by a long shot."

"I know." Gil sounded almost sad. "Come with me. We need to get to Jeltor."

"Agreed." Barnabas stood. "How are we going to get him to the ship, by the way?"

"There's a spare tank we can use." Gil led the way down the hall. "I think we probably *don't* want him to be in a biosuit he can move around in."

"You're really worried he's been converted." Barnabas made himself say the words.

When Gil said nothing, Barnabas felt dread settle into the pit of his stomach.

Gar made his way down the stairs almost silently. He had thought that combat training would be all learning how to hit things, but Barnabas had made Gar learn all sorts of other skills as well: marksmanship, throwing, moving silently, and more. Gar tried to practice another lesson as he walked: paying attention to every sound he heard.

When he reached the door at the bottom of the stairs, he paused and listened closely. He did not hear anything moving outside, so he eased the door open as quietly as he could and closed it behind himself. Then he slipped down the hallway to the records room, gun at the ready.

It was good that he had because he was about halfway to the records room when the guard Shinigami had heard came back into the hallway.

Gar didn't hesitate. He broke into a full-on sprint, a roar bursting from his lips. *Shinigami—wait and choose your moment!*

Will do. She sounded amused. *Your battle cries are ridiculous, you know.*

I know. Gar gave a small smile of satisfaction as his opponent started running as well. *But he has to think I'm committing to this. One moment.*

As they ran, the Jotun leveled one arm at Gar, and Gar's newly-enhanced vision picked out the gleam of a tiny needle. The Jotuns really did love their poisons and needles. It didn't matter, however, because Gar hadn't ever intended to tackle his opponent. Instead, as he drew close, he took two long, loping steps—and leapt over the Jotun's head.

The Jotun gave a mechanical squawk of surprise as Gar flipped in midair. He managed to swing around quickly but hadn't yet readied another weapon when Gar aimed his pistol and shot twice in succession.

The Jotuns weren't stupid. Their biosuits were designed to be bulletproof. They hadn't had much contact with the Etheric Empire, however, and Gar's bullets caused a spiderweb of cracks across the tank. The Jotun flailed and gave an angry yell. Blades appeared on its arms, and armor plating shot forward to close around the internal tank.

In the confusion, Shinigami wrenched open the door to the records room and threw the dead Jotun at the new attacker, sending him staggering sideways.

Ice-cold, Gar told her.

His career is helping people take over the world with mind-control and torture. Shinigami strode out into the hall, her face set in an expression that made Gar never want to mess with her.

You know, that's a good point. He brought one leg up and kicked the Jotun to keep it off-balance, then pivoted and dropped his shoulder, whipping the leg around in a circle and slamming his heel into the biosuit's head. The Jotun dropped to its knees.

"Who are you?" the Jotun yelled. "A *Luvendi?*" It looked at Shinigami. "And a human. *Barnabas.*"

Shinigami stood her ground as it leapt up and tried to charge her, and her fist shot out at the last moment. Instead of fragile bone and flesh there was metal and reinforced biotic skin, and her punch dented the armor plating around the tank. An ominous crack sounded from inside.

"So close," Shinigami said, "and yet so far."

The Jotun leapt into motion, slashing at her, driving her back with strikes and kicks, and Shinigami ducked and tried to find her way through the flurry of strikes. All of the cuts on her arms opened bloodlessly.

Gar watched, not wanting to intervene too quickly. Shinigami was competent at sparring; more than competent, really. She simply did not have the base of knowledge yet that most species had about how she could move and where her body was in space.

She struck with her fists, knees, and elbows and created a series of impressive dents in the Jotun's suit.

And then it drew back and cocked its head to the side. One hand was clenched around her wrist.

"Aha," it said. "A biosuit of some sort, and you don't know how to fight in it yet."

Gar's reflexes had been enhanced, but even he had

trouble following what happened next. The two combatants moved in a flicker of strikes executed so fast that their limbs were a blur. Shinigami, when push came to shove, had abandoned the traditional tempo of the fight and was lashing out as quickly as her programming would allow.

Gar gave a whoop. *"Yeah!"*

He was able to see the Jotun stagger sideways across the hall, and from the angle, she must have backhanded it in the face. There was a strange smell in the air and fluid was leaking from its chest.

"You have him on the ropes, Shinigami!" Gar wasn't entirely sure what that phrase referred to, but Tabitha used it every so often.

Unfortunately, the Jotun had realized the same thing—and it was prepared for that eventuality. A cloud of smoke billowed from its body, causing Gar's skin and lungs to burn. He doubled over in agony. Electrical current buzzed, and Shinigami cried out. A moment later, there was the pounding of feet and the slam of a door.

Their opponent was gone.

Feword staggered up the stairs, trying not to panic.

The humans were here, and they weren't what he'd thought. For one thing, the human he'd been fighting was actually biotic. Were *all* of them biotic? He had no idea. For years, humans had seemed to be creatures of flesh and blood, but what if that had been a ruse?

All that mattered was Jeltor, he reminded himself. He had to get there before the humans did.

Because if the ship nearby was the *Shinigami*, it was too much of a coincidence for them to be here. They knew Jeltor had been taken for conversion. Who else knew, Feword could not be sure—but his duty was clear. He needed to get the asset out and to a safe place.

He just wasn't sure if he could make it. His suit was leaking steadily, and he hunkered down against the bottom of his tank as the fluid dipped lower. How had that Luvendi's weapons managed to crack his tank? And how could the human possibly have hit him hard enough to do further damage?

Feword was rarely angry, but he was angry now. Grisor was seeking to accomplish great things, and these humans —these lesser beings—were trying to stand in the way.

He wasn't going to allow that.

He made it to one of the control panels on the wall and leaned there for a moment, struggling to breathe properly. The fluid wasn't retaining oxygen the way it should.

That meant he had to move *faster*, not rest here. His suit's arm came up and attached to the control panel, working its way into the sensor array and then unleashing a series of commands. There was another human, yes, and it was with…Gil.

Of course. Too late, everything became clear. Gil hadn't been holding back from converting Jeltor because he was worried about the captain breaking. He hadn't been a scientist at all. Feword could have kicked himself.

Take out Gil and Wev, he instructed over the personal channel in his suit.

Only one reply came back, from Yeldred: *I saw Wev going up to the alien cages. I will deal with him.*

Be careful, Feword replied. He wanted to scream his frustration. *I believe Boltar and Jilrun are dead.*

There was a pause, and then Yeldred recovered his composure. *And Jeltor?*

I'm getting Jeltor, Feword replied. *They're not going to win.*

CHAPTER TWENTY-TWO

Barnabas! Gar's tone was panicked. *It got away from us. And Shinigami—*

What's wrong? Barnabas fought the urge to stop or turn around. He had to keep moving. Gar said their target had gotten away from them, not that they were in the middle of a bad fight.

I'm fine. Shinigami sounded furious. *Our opponent knew how to deal with cybernetic bodies, that's all. I should have guessed he would. He managed to keep me motionless for a few moments while Gar was dealing with the poison gas.*

We're following his path since he's leaking fluid, Gar added. *But—*

Poison gas? Barnabas interrupted. He pressed a button to flip his helmet into place, and it appeared around him as if materializing out of thin air. In reality the super-light material had been stored in a collar around his neck, but the effect was impressive. *No, if he can neutralize you both, stay back.*

"What's going on?" Gil asked him.

"We need to move quickly," Barnabas explained. "The guard who went downstairs got away from Gar and Shinigami. I'd guess he's going for the most valuable asset on site, wouldn't you?"

Gil nodded, and his pace quickened. "This way, then. We need to get up two more flights before he does, and I don't know which way he's going."

They had only gone a few more yards, however, before there was the unmistakable click of all of the doors on the floor locking.

Barnabas swore internally with the sort of inventiveness that only a multilingual devotee of Bethany Anne could summon. He grabbed one of the nearby doors and had to be pushed away the next moment. The doors were electrified.

"I should have heard the hum," he muttered, embarrassed.

The truth was, he *had* heard the hum, and he'd been so angry that he'd wanted to yank the door off its hinges anyway. His fury at his opponent and his fear for Jeltor were getting the better of him. He needed to get a handle on himself *now*.

Shinigami, is Gar okay?

He's all right, Shinigami said soothingly. *I got his helmet on him, and he's breathing good air now. All healed, no damage.*

Excellent, thank you. To Gar, he said, *Is Shinigami okay?*

She seems to be doing fine, Gar reported. *I was worried, but she's recovered and is muttering about how next time he's going to get a nasty surprise.*

Good, thank you. He was satisfied that since he hadn't

asked them about themselves, both were telling the truth, Barnabas looked around and considered, then he took a running start and brought his rubber-soled boot up to smash the door at the end of the hallway off its hinges. He stared at it, panting, as it clattered down the stairs.

"Come on," he called to Gil. "You said we had to go up two flights."

"Yes." Gil caught up quickly. "I didn't know you could do that."

"Most humans can't," Barnabas explained. "However, I —actually, you know what? You work in Jotun Intelligence, I think I'll avoid giving you details."

"Have it your way, but if you're referring to the fact that Queen Bethany Anne and some of her inner circle are enhanced in some ways, that's hardly new information." Gil sounded untroubled. "She fought King Yoll in single combat, and there have been numerous stories about— what is his name, John Grimes? Yes. And others. But if all humans could do such things, I think we would have heard about that."

Barnabas grunted noncommittally, taking the stairs three at a time. He was hardly going to go out of his way to confirm what so far was only conjecture on Gil's part. The Jotuns had already gone a bit crazy with enhancement, in his opinion, and he wasn't going to give them any more ideas.

At the door to the floor that housed Jeltor, they could again hear the electrical hum, and Barnabas sighed as he considered his options. He had no real space to build up steam here, and the door was set to open into the stairwell, not out of it—meaning that he would need to strike it far, far harder to break it.

And time was ticking away. With a snarl, Barnabas whirled away. "Who else could help us?"

"My partner, but he's not on this floor." Gil hesitated, then became quiet. Barnabas guessed he was communicating internally, and that guess was confirmed when Gil said, "I asked him to help. He says he will."

"How much time?" Barnabas asked tensely.

"He'll do it as fast as possible," Gil said. "That's the best I can tell you."

"I don't need your best," Barnabas shot back, "I need Jeltor saved."

"No," Gil said. "You know very well that what we *need* is for the committee *not* to achieve its goals. As important as Jeltor is to you, he's a secondary concern."

Wev hurried down the long corridor that lay between the rows of cages. Some of the aliens came forward to snarl at him, others to plead for mercy—at least, so he assumed. Many of them could no longer speak in any way he understood. The Brakalon did not say anything to him. He only cried, as he always did.

Soon you'll be free, Wev promised them silently. They couldn't hear him, but he needed to say it to stay sane.

Getting them out would be difficult. The facility had not been made to transport captives to and from ships. Either they left converted and ready to serve the committee, or they were killed. If the facility were breached, there were self-destruct implants throughout the entire building.

The thought filled Wev with utter hatred. The committee believed that everything should serve their purpose or be destroyed. There was no middle ground.

While Gil was taking out the guards one by one, Wev would be preparing the experiments to load them into the ship. He had already done the preliminary work to make Jeltor easy to transport. The captain had been transferred to a smaller tank and could easily be removed from the laboratory.

Now, Wev was focusing on the other experiments. Since the ship they had brought was small and had limited secured space, that meant preparing a *lot* of tranquilizers. They would need to keep the experiments unconscious as long as possible

Wev. Gil's voice echoed through his suit. *I need your help. Humans are here to rescue Jeltor, but one of the guards has locked us off that floor.*

What? Which guard?

Does it matter? I need you to get to a control panel and get us access.

Wev swore, but he knew better than to argue. If one of the guards was trying to get to Jeltor, there was no saying what they might do. If it was Feword and he had figured out how to use the trigger words on Jeltor...

The whole Navy could be compromised. Cursing, Wev ran as fast as his biosuit would take him, coming out into the main corridor while the experiments called after him in desperation.

His fear and distraction were nearly fatal. A punch

caught him on the side of his sensor array and knocked his suit sideways. Yeldred, armed and armored far better than Wev could ever hope to be, stepped out of the shadows with a ripple of satisfaction.

"Setting the experiments free, traitor?"

"I don't know what you're talking about." Behind him, Wev could see the control panel winking, so he did the only thing he could think of. He held up his tentacles in a gesture of surrender. "What's going on? Why are you attacking me? Are you with the Navy?"

"Am *I* with the Navy?" Yeldred hissed back. He had always been the meanest of the guards, often threatening to kill the experiments when they disturbed his sleep. Now, he readied a blade and a gun as he stared Wev down. "When your partner is the one killing guards?"

"He did *what*?" Wev shot back, trying to make himself sound as shocked as possible. Then, in the split-second Yeldred considered this, Wev unveiled the gun he kept well-hidden in his arm plating and shot.

Sparks burst across Yeldred's sensor array, and he staggered back with a yell. Wev shot again, denting Yeldred's gun, and then ran around him to the control panel. He plugged in, keeping his sensor array trained on Yeldred as the guard tried to regain his equilibrium.

Feword was the one who had shut down Jeltor's floor. Wev struggled through the blocks, trying to undo them, cursing when he saw how Feword had locked everyone else out of the system. Wev knew the overrides, but they weren't going to be quick...

Wev! Any progress?

Wev was slammed up against the wall. Yeldred had

recovered, and his knives bit into the joints of Wev's armor.

Yeldred...here...

Wev!

Have to get Jeltor out, Wev managed. He kicked back and tried to level an elbow strike at Yeldred's head, but he didn't take his other arm out of the panel. He was devoting as much attention as he could to getting around Feword's blocks. *Soon...I'll have it done...* Another hit, and he felt a searing agony in his Jotun body. The suit was made to tell him when it was injured, and it was badly injured now. *Soon,* he repeated.

Wev, get out of there!

Yeldred was laughing. "You're going to die, traitor. You and Gil, and I'm going to enjoy showing your bodies to His Excellency."

"You...sure about that?" Wev gasped, and he unblocked one part of the system Feword hadn't gotten to yet.

Nearby, the cage doors swung open, and the captive Brakalon bellowed. Yeldred swore, turning to look as the experiments streamed around the corner and saw him standing there, weapons out.

Yeldred had a gun, but they didn't care. They rushed him, screaming and desperate for vengeance, and Wev did his best to stay upright and conscious while he waded through the last of Feword's blocks.

Gil...

Wev! Wev, are you all right?

It's...done. Go get him. Wev dropped to his knees, pulling his arm out of the wall panel, and the last thing he saw was the world tilting crazily as the Brakalon picked his biosuit up gently from the floor.

"Wev!" Gil's voice was full of agony.

Barnabas didn't wait. He couldn't. He wrenched the door open as soon as the hum disappeared and ran down the corridors. To any organic being, he would be only a blur.

Jeltor, please! Please be all right. He skidded around the corner into the big central room, terrified of what he would see and hear.

But the big tank was empty, and the wet tracks across the floor showed him that another tank had been wheeled away.

When he felt the low thrum of engines nearby, Barnabas realized they were too late.

CHAPTER TWENTY-THREE

Shinigami! Barnabas took the stairs down to the ground floor at top speed, grabbing the handrails to swing himself around. He would have dropped straight down through the center, but the Jotun architects hadn't left nearly enough room for that. *Fire up the ship! We're going now!*

Engines are on, she reported. *Problem, though... One of our allies is dead, and the other one is walking right into it—*

No time!

I'm not finished, Shinigami said severely. *The live one is walking into a trap, and the committee must know what's going on because they have this place on a self-destruct. As long as I'm here, I can stave it off, but once we leave...*

Not our problem.

Do you even hear yourself? She was angry now. *Our allies here are why we had a fighting chance to get to Jeltor. We can catch that ship, even with a few minutes more of a head start. What we* can't *do is resurrect our allies from tiny exploded bits!*

I can't— Barnabas gave a yell of fury and spun to slam his fist into the wall as he skidded to a halt. *Goddammit! We were supposed to get him, Shinigami. This was supposed to be—*

He stopped and stood for a moment, his chest heaving.

There was a pause, and then she said quietly in his mind, *May I speak as a friend?*

Barnabas swallowed. *Yes. Always.*

Something about this enemy has hooked deep into you. All trace of joking was gone. *Please, for this one, let me call the shots when I say I need to. I promise you that I will not sacrifice our friends.*

Barnabas stood frozen for a long moment. Months ago, he would never have considered letting Shinigami pick their targets and formulate their plans. Of course, a few months ago, she would never have suggested going out of their way to save their allies, and her plans for infiltration would have involved missiles and flamethrowers.

She had changed…and so had he.

Barnabas, please! You have to trust me. Gil doesn't have much time.

He felt farther from logic and reason than he had in years, and he clung to her voice as a bastion of sanity. *I'm going now. Up two flights, yes?*

Yes. She sounded relieved. *I'm getting Gar to the ship unless you think you'll need him.*

No. You two go. Barnabas was taking the stairs three at a time, pulling himself around corners as he had gone down, his mind narrowing to the task ahead: get Gil out.

When he burst onto the top floor, it was with a battle cry on his lips and murder in his eyes. Gil was injured badly, his movements jerky, sparks raining down from his suit, but he wasn't backing down from his fight with the Jotun soldier. He screamed his friend's name over and over as he fought.

Around them, the experiments lay wounded and dying. Barnabas guessed that these aliens were the only reason Gil stood a fighting chance. It looked as if they had attacked in a mob and had done significant damage to the soldier's biosuit. They weren't strong, however, and most of them bore such brutal wounds, inflicted head on, that it looked like they had no longer been safe enough to do anything other than charge their captors in a fit of rage.

And there, on the side of the room, was a Brakalon taking its last breaths. As it died, Barnabas heard the keening sound of its cry and remembered what he had heard in the entryway of the facility. The cry was full of so much pain and loss that he could hardly help seeing into the creature's memories: the destruction of its home, the death of its family, the torture it had endured.

Something inside Barnabas snapped.

The committee's lackey never stood a chance. From his perspective, Barnabas moved in a blur. The punch Barnabas leveled at him was hard enough to punch through the armor plating on the front of his suit. His tank exploded within the armor shell, and the Jotun's body was smashed against the back wall.

Gil staggered back in shock as Barnabas ripped the suit limb from limb, a wordless roar bursting out of his chest. When it was done, when the suit was nothing more than a sparking ruin, he stared at it with his chest heaving and his hands twitching, aching for something more to hit, to tear, to destroy.

He staggered back to the Brakalon and knelt. His bloody fingers, coated with the slime from inside the Jotun's tank, reached out to brush the creature's face.

Rest, he told it. He found the memories of its family, living and happy, and he brought those to the surface of its mind. *You don't have to fight anymore. Rest.*

He felt its happiness for one blessed moment, and then the pain released entirely and its head fell back onto the floor.

Barnabas. Whether Shinigami could see what he was seeing he did not know, but her voice was sober. *The records are loaded, and we should go now. They're stepping up their attempts at a self-destruct.*

Barnabas stood. He was unutterably weary now, and he wanted nothing more than to be gone from this place. He looked at Gil, who was kneeling by Wev's body.

"Come," he told the Jotun. "We have to go. There's nothing left here."

Gil came with him as if in a dream, stumbling a little as he walked. He didn't speak while Barnabas led him into the stairwell and down the three flights. He walked numbly past the body of the Jotun guard outside the records room, and he did not look around at all while Barnabas hurried him onto the *Shinigami* and they braced for takeoff.

But when they heard the alert to tell them they had left the atmosphere, Gil stirred to life at last. His mechanical face turned to Barnabas and he said, his voice flat and lost, "It should have been me."

Feword slumped into the pilot's seat and shook with rage. The repair module in the ship had done its job well. The leaking from his tank had stopped, the fluid was replenished, and the rest of his suit…

It would hold until he could get proper repairs done by a master mechanic on one of their bases. That would have to do for now. There was nothing to do in the meantime except try to relax—

An automated system of alerts sprang to life a moment later, wailing throughout the ship. In the tank nearby, Jeltor was startled awake. He thrashed, blinded and crippled by the torture, but his terror soon gave way to exhaustion and he floated limply, realizing he was helpless.

Feword gave him a contemptuous look before turning to look at the ship's control panel. He knew what the alerts were without looking, but he still stared at the sensor arrays for a long moment.

The *Shinigami* was in pursuit. He simply had to hope he could make it to Jotuna D before they caught up with him. The ship was already traveling at its top speed. Fiddling with it would help nothing.

Feword resisted the urge to stride across the bridge and shatter Jeltor's tank. This traitor, this upstart captain, had cost him his whole team—and the research facility.

Feword hoped he was worth it.

Barnabas helped Gil to the shuttle bay, where Shinigami was waiting with tools. Gil stood without a word of protest —or, indeed, any sign that he was still conscious—while

Shinigami's exquisitely-calibrated hands repaired the tiny cracks in his tank and the multitude of wires and joints that powered his biosuit.

"It isn't as good as it would be if a Jotun mechanic had done it," she said when she was done. "Not all of the weapons panels will work properly. We're formulating more fluid to put into the tank. Gar will be here with it soon."

The mechanical head nodded once.

Barnabas had been pacing near the door, his hands linked behind his back, and now he looked at Gil. What would he be feeling if it were Gar or Shinigami who had been lost in that facility? He could not imagine.

"Do you need to go anywhere urgently?" he asked at last.

Gil said nothing for long enough for Barnabas to wonder if he'd switched off his sensor arrays and retreated into his Jotun body.

"No," he said finally, tonelessly. "I've informed Intelligence of what happened. There is no more we can do. I will have to go back to the Agency."

Barnabas and Shinigami exchanged a look.

"They're not going to hurt you, are they?" Shinigami asked finally. She was always willing to be blunter than a human would be in her place.

"No!" Gil's tone betrayed genuine shock. He looked at her as Gar and Tafa hurried in with a closed container of fluid. "Why would you think that?"

"One too many bad experiences," Barnabas answered for Shinigami. "We've seen a great number of people be punished for things that were beyond their control."

Gil began to laugh. He laughed wildly, the sound cutting off as Shinigami eased his tank forward for Gar to pour the fluid in; the sound came back when the tank was settled into place once more, bouncing off the walls. It was disturbing in its intensity.

"What more could they do to punish me?" Gil finally asked. "Wev is dead. What could they do that's worse than that? No, my punishment is my failure."

"You didn't fail," Barnabas assured him quietly.

"I asked him to go!" Gil yelled. His voice clipped against the range of the speakers, raw in its grief. "I was the one who said he needed to stop what he was doing and get Jeltor out—and we didn't!"

"We're going to get him back," Shinigami told him softly. She opened her mouth to say more but caught Barnabas' minute head shake. She closed her mouth again.

"Gil," Barnabas began, "I know that no words can bring Wev back."

Gil stared at him, and Barnabas could feel the hatred roiling in Gil's mind. How *dare* Barnabas even *speak* to him, when Wev had died for Barnabas' mission, and Barnabas had his whole crew around him, alive and safe?

"Both you and Wev were prepared to give everything to stop the committee," Barnabas said gravely. "To stop your own government from becoming something truly horrific. Wev did nothing less than what you would have done in his place." He paused. "I imagine...well, I imagine neither of you thought you would get out of this mission alive."

Gil stared at him wordlessly.

"Wev paid the price you expected to pay," Barnabas said, "but you're still alive. I know it's too soon right now, but I hope you will continue to fight. The committee is not defeated yet, Gil. The Jotuns still need you."

Gil looked down at the ground.

"Gilwar," he said finally. "That's my full name."

"Gilwar," Barnabas repeated. "We'll leave you in peace. Speak up if you need anything. Shinigami will hear you."

He waved the others out of the shuttle bay and lagged behind them as they made their way to the bridge. He wasn't surprised to see Shinigami turn to look at him from down the hall.

Do you want to talk about it? The question was awkward, but the fact that she'd asked it at all made him smile.

Not...yet. There were too many thoughts for him to articulate any of them. *I'm going to shower, and then I'll come to the bridge. Let's see if we can capture this ship before they get wherever they're going.*

Jotuna D is my guess, Shinigami said. *And I'm doing what I can.* She looked at him for another moment, then turned and walked toward the Pod-doc that had been formulated to fix her cybernetic skin.

Barnabas watched her go, then went to his quarters.

Trust me, Shinigami had said. He could do that. He had to.

She was right. Something had hooked deep into him with this case. Without his team, he would be lost.

CHAPTER TWENTY-FOUR

"Barnabas?" Shinigami's voice echoed around the room as Barnabas finished buttoning his shirt.

He paused. "Yes?" His heart was suddenly beating very quickly.

"We're pursuing, and not far out from Jotuna D. I have not been able to disrupt any of their systems so that we could land. I'm worried that if we try to force it, they will simply kill Jeltor." She paused, and he could sense her choosing her words carefully. "My recommendation would be to keep following the ship without engaging."

She placed faint stress on the word *recommendation,* and he sensed that she was looking for his input. Shinigami, it seemed, did not enjoy command.

Barnabas smiled slightly before remembering that she could probably see him. "I think your reasoning is sound," he said. "I'm willing to go with your judgment on this. I trust you."

She made a sound like a spoon in a garbage disposal,

leaving Barnabas wondering what exactly she'd meant to convey. Privately, he thought that she might be a little nervous about running a mission.

Since they had begun working together, she had *definitely* changed—more than he had realized, in fact.

"We'll be in range of the moon in forty-five minutes," Shinigami told him, apparently having recovered her composure. "I'll know at that point if they're going to be landing there. I'll tell you if anything happens before then."

"Thank you."

Barnabas studied himself in the mirror for a moment before combing his hair carefully. He selected a tie, knotted it, and pulled on a vest. This was a useless gesture, as he might need to change into armor again in short order, but putting on clean, neat clothes made him feel like himself.

He had not felt like himself for some time now.

He worked hard to think of nothing as he cleaned his armor and his weapons, taking care not to get any grease or blood on his clothing. He laid everything out once more when he was finished, looked at it in satisfaction, and washed his hands thoroughly. After the time spent doing these tasks, he felt calmer.

"You should come to the bridge," Shinigami said suddenly.

His calm vanished. Shinigami did not tend to speak like that unless there was a good reason. Barnabas left his armor laid out and headed for the bridge at a brisk walk, trying to retain a sense of process and decorum. Halfway there, he broke into a run and arrived at the same time as Gar and Tafa.

Barnabas stepped back to allow them onto the bridge

first. Discipline, he believed, was made of small moments like this, forcing himself to stillness when he wanted to rush to his seat—as if it would help.

That was when the ship banked sharply. Alarms went off and Tafa gave a worried cry, sliding into her seat and bringing up all of her panels. Gar, who had gripped his chair to keep from falling, threw a hand out to steady Barnabas, and in her seat, Shinigami fixed her eyes on the screen with grim determination.

"Shinigami?" Barnabas crossed the room quickly, giving Gar a nod of thanks, and sat to study the view screens. Missiles and energy beams of some sort were streaking past them, and from the flicker on the screens at the side of the room, concerted attacks were being made on their cloaking and other internal processes.

"Jotuna D," Shinigami said, sounding annoyed, "has a defense system that rivals High Tortuga's."

Barnabas turned to look at the screen again. The Jotun ship was not far ahead of them, although it was moving more quickly than Barnabas would have thought possible. Of all species he had personally encountered, the Jotuns were the most dangerous in terms of technology.

Until recently, he would have said they were less dangerous than other species because they did not have imperial ambitions. Now, however, he was not so sure. Whether or not the committee enjoyed broad support, Jotun society had produced a dedicated and well-funded group that was hell-bent on subjugating the rest of this sector.

That said something.

A new storm of beeping arose, and the screen automatically highlighted several small objects that had been launched toward them by a satellite. Barnabas frowned at them.

"What *are* those?"

"Bots," Tafa said.

"Do you have any idea what they do?"

"Override our systems, shut down our life support, and vent the ship," said a new voice.

Everyone turned to look at the doorway, where Gil stood with his mechanical face pointing at the screens.

"I see," Barnabas said. "Shinigami—"

"Already taken care of." Shinigami settled back in her seat and gave a small smile. "Pucks."

"Ah." Barnabas smiled as he watched the red-high-lighted shapes explode one by one and disappear from the tracking systems.

"I'd almost like to get one to study," Shinigami said in an undertone.

"No," Barnabas said flatly.

"Oh, come on, we could—"

"He's right. You shouldn't allow any of the committee's technology on board," Gil said. He stepped onto the bridge and paused. "May I enter?"

"That's supposed to be my line," Barnabas murmured. When everyone looked at him in confusion, he rolled his eyes. "Vampire joke, never mind."

"Hey, he's back." Shinigami smiled at him. "Bad jokes and all."

"I do not make *bad* jokes."

"Yes, you do. All the time. Until recently." She jerked her head at Gil. "And what about this guy?"

"Ah, yes." Barnabas nodded to Gil. "Please, come in. We've followed the ship to Jotuna D."

Gil came a few steps into the room. His eyes focused on the moon. "I believe Senator Grisor has an estate there."

"That sounds about right." Barnabas narrowed his eyes. "I wonder if he'd be so bold as to have Jeltor taken there, although he must know that we're onto him by—"

"Everybody brace!" Shinigami yelled. A new spread of missiles had just launched, and the ship flung itself into a dizzying array of maneuvers. The planet swung wildly and disappeared in the view screen and Barnabas looked away, fighting for control of his stomach.

Something must have clipped them because the ship went spinning sideways as Shinigami swore under her breath.

"If I can just get us through this layer—"

"There's another layer of satellites in extremely low orbit," Gil reported.

"You have got to be kidding me! What *is* this place?"

"Many senators have homes here. It's considered a very fashionable place for them, so it's armed to the teeth, I believe humans would say."

Barnabas looked at the missiles that were circling them and at the satellites that still had not been taken out, and envisaged another layer of satellites and whatever antiaircraft measures were on the surface. "Shinigami, get out of here."

"*What?*" She stared at him incredulously. "No way. No. You can't be serious." The ship swerved again, and her fingers tightened on the armrest to hold herself in place. "We're so close, and if we don't see where he's landing—"

"Shinigami, you asked me to trust you." Barnabas held her eyes. "I did. Now it's time to trust *me*. We aren't going to get Jeltor back if we're in a bunch of bloody pieces in orbit."

Shinigami hesitated—though, thankfully, her hesitation was limited to this decision. The ship continued to maneuver without a pause.

She looked back at the screen and grimaced. "*Fine*. But I'm torching some of these stupid-ass things on the way out."

"You do that." Barnabas crossed one knee over the other and sat back. He watched as pucks took out three of the satellites and sent another reeling out of position, and he noted from the stream of information crossing the screens nearby that Shinigami was collecting as much data as she could on their internal systems.

"Is...*she* flying the ship?" Gil asked Barnabas quietly. "She looks away from her controls quite frequently."

"It's complicated," Barnabas said. As the ship spun partially out of control, he added, "*Shinigami*, what was that?"

"A damned sight better than you'd be doing in my place, I'll tell you that." She gave him a grin.

"I don't dispute that, but— Well, to cut to the chase, how much is Helen going to yell at me when we go in for maintenance next time?"

Shinigami snickered, which was not, in Barnabas' opinion, a heartening sign. He sighed and rubbed his temples.

"Well, that was disappointing."

Gil was staring at him in confusion. "I didn't think you were generally so...calm...about setbacks."

"Your first experience with me was somewhat atypical." Barnabas stood. "All right, we'll all meet in the conference room in one hour. Until then, brainstorm on your own about how to get onto that planet. We have to get there soon, and we need to go in silent. Not only that, this may be a larger base of operations. Gil, we'll need any information you have on it."

Gil nodded.

"Where are you going?" Shinigami asked Barnabas.

"To call Carter," Barnabas said. "We're going to be going back on High Tortuga later than I said, so I should definitely tell him. It's only polite. Also, I will need beer when I get there, I can already tell."

CHAPTER TWENTY-FIVE

"**B**arnabas." Carter appeared on the screen, suntanned and grinning. "Heading our way?"

"Not just yet." Barnabas smiled back. It was impossible not to. Carter was the type of person whose good moods were irrepressible and absolutely infectious. He'd be the perfect person to be stuck on a desert island with... assuming you didn't kill him for being so damned cheery about the whole experience. "We have a loose end to tie up, and I really don't know how long it's going to take."

Carter nodded in easy understanding. "In your line of work you can never tell, can you?"

"I wanted to apologize," Barnabas explained. "I doubt I'll be back before your niece leaves." In his head, he saw a smile very much like Carter's and had a pang of something that felt surprisingly like regret. He would have enjoyed talking in circles with Aliana, making her panic that he'd figured out her game and then pretending he had no idea.

To his surprise, Carter looked very pleased with himself. "Actually, Aliana will be staying for a while."

"Really?" Barnabas' brows went up. "I thought she had…a job."

"Oh, she did," Carter said. He still looked like the cat that had the cream. "I pointed out that cargo handlers are a dime a dozen. No offense to Aliana, of course; I'm sure she was a damned fine employee, but it's not like they'll have trouble replacing her."

"Of course," Barnabas replied, deriving secret amusement from the fact that Carter seemed to have no idea what Aliana's job had actually been. "So she quit, did she? Interesting. I wonder why?"

To his surprise, Carter looked almost evasive for a moment. "I, uh… Well, she's staying to help with Elisa's pregnancy. Look after the twins, work at the bar. You know, all that stuff."

"Oh?" Barnabas frowned slightly.

"You know how hard being pregnant is. Well, you've heard, I'm sure."

Barnabas, who had indeed heard multiple soliloquies on the subject from Gabrielle, nodded blandly. Then his frown deepened. "I thought Elisa was doing well? There's not a problem, is there? Because we could probably get her over to one of the bigger hospitals if we needed to. In fact—"

"No, no, it's…ah…" Carter rubbed at his hair, then shook his head. "So what's this complication that came up in your mission?"

Barnabas allowed himself to be led but resolved to circle back around to this topic. It was unlike Carter to be evasive, and if something actually was wrong with Elisa, Barnabas wanted to know it.

"There's… Oh, hell, where to start?"

"I don't think I've ever heard you say 'hell,'" Carter exclaimed, sounding impressed. "It *must* be serious."

"How much do you know about the Jotuns?" Barnabas asked him.

"Uh…about the normal amount, I'd guess. They wear mechanical suits, they seem to be fairly reclusive. Wait—it was the Jotuns you fought with, right? Against the Yennai Corporation."

"Some of them." Barnabas sighed. "The Navy. The Senate was in the Yennai Corporation's pocket."

"Better than the other way around, right?"

"I— Well, yes. I hadn't thought of it like that." Barnabas felt his lips twitch. He hadn't smiled nearly enough lately. He struggled to hold onto the feeling as he spoke again. "Another portion of the Senate—a committee—came up with this insane plan…"

In the shadows of the hallway, Aliana took a careful step closer to the door. She hadn't come up here to eavesdrop; she wouldn't do that. She'd heard her name, though, and that had stopped her in her tracks. And then she'd heard Barnabas' voice, and *that* had made her want to hear what was going on.

They were talking about her? *Her?* The thought of it made her feel very odd.

And then she remembered just why Barnabas might be

interested in her, and absolute panic filled her. She edged down the hallway as quietly as she could, her need to hear what was going on at odds with the creakiness of the floorboards.

Carter was competent when it came to building things. The bar was hardly going to fall down anytime soon. It was just that it creaked a lot.

To her disappointment, by the time she reached the door they were talking about something else entirely. She frowned as she listened in, biting her lip.

"So they were abducting civilians from these remote border colonies," Barnabas was saying. "Huword always tortured a few himself. I think he just liked doing it, honestly."

Her uncle said nothing to this, but Aliana knew him well enough to guess that he was torn between horror and fury. She knew, because it was the feeling that was currently roiling in her own chest. The two of them had always reacted similarly when it came to things like this.

Barnabas must have realized this because he said quietly, "I don't have to tell you all of it. You know."

"No." Carter sounded resolute. "I want to know. I *have* to know what's out there now, because—" He didn't finish the sentence.

"*No one* like that will get to you on High Tortuga." Barnabas' reply was unequivocal. "Any fleet goes near that planet, it will be in tiny pieces within minutes. I promise you that, Carter."

There was a pause, and Aliana leaned closer to see what her uncle was doing. He was staring at the floor, his shoulders hunched, but he nodded.

"Thank you," he said quietly, and then, "Tell me. Why would anyone... Why would they do that?"

Barnabas hesitated, and Aliana wished she could see the screen.

"Mind control," he said finally. "They were testing a process that would make sentient beings loyal to them. Whether they perfected it for other species, I couldn't say. There were...test subjects...in the laboratory we found, but they weren't in good shape. They did figure it out for their own kind."

"They were doing it to their *own* people?" Carter was furious now. Horror was gone; there was only anger.

"They knew that the Navy would oppose them. They must have suspected that the civilians would do the same. I don't think they have the technology to do it on a mass scale, not yet, but..."

He took a deep breath and Aliana clenched her hands. So this was the sort of thing Barnabas did, and the type of people he stopped. She had known about the Rangers, but she'd only had a vague idea what they did. She had never heard examples.

She wished she still hadn't. She felt sick to her stomach and then totally fine, by turns—because it couldn't be real, could it? No one would do that.

Except, apparently they would.

"But they have Jeltor," Barnabas said finally.

Carter made a sound of surprise and his feet, which had been propped on the desk, thudded to the ground. "Your friend? The one you rescued with Tafa?"

Barnabas must have nodded. He didn't speak.

"Barnabas." Carter sounded like he didn't know what to

say. "Is he... Are you all right? Is *he*— Of course, he's not all right. I don't know why I..."

"He might be," Barnabas replied softly. Aliana could hear him clinging to hope. "They've only had a little time to work on him, so he might still be...himself. But he might not be." It took courage for him to say those words. "I don't know what to expect," he said almost to himself. "I don't know what it will look like, or even what they wanted to happen. It would be subtle; it would have to be, for him to be a sleeper agent. What if he lies to me?"

Carter leaned his elbows on his knees and let Barnabas talk. Aliana watched his familiar profile for a moment and had a memory, unexpected, of skinning her knees on the ground at one of the parks on the *Meredith Reynolds,* and Carter holding her hand while the skin healed, and she sniffled. He was like that. He just listened when you needed him to.

Barnabas sighed again. "Tell me honestly. Is Elisa all right?"

"She's fine," Carter said absently. Then, coming back to himself, he groaned. "I...may have exaggerated things when I was trying to get Aliana to stay."

In the shadows, Aliana froze.

Barnabas said nothing, but Aliana guessed he must have looked disapproving because Carter threw his hands up.

"I didn't know what to *do*," he protested. "She—her husband— Okay, well, *ex*-husband, I think... Huh."

"I don't think I got any of that," Barnabas told him frankly. "Start again."

"I don't even know where to start." Carter sighed.

Aliana wanted to run. Every part of her was screaming

for her to do so, but she just couldn't seem to move. She squeezed her eyes shut, but that didn't keep the words from making their way into her skull.

"She got married at nineteen," Carter explained. "No, no, it's not like that, not like you're thinking. Harry was great. He really was. Everyone was all upset that they got married so young, but when you saw them together, it made sense. They went all over together, like Elisa and me." He paused and swallowed. "And then Harry died. It was sudden in a way, but drawn out enough to be... I can't even imagine, Barnabas. She doesn't talk about it. I know a little. I can imagine more, and that's enough to make me want to —I don't even know. To watch someone you love waste away and not be able to help..."

Through the tears, streaming silently down Aliana's cheeks, she heard Barnabas say, "I know."

And he did. She could tell. He *did* know.

Carter took a deep breath to steady himself. "Lawrence was a mistake. He was her second husband. She did it... well, she did it when she was still cut up over Harry. She wanted to forget everything, I think, and he screwed her over good. He took her ship. I just want..."

Barnabas waited.

"I want her to be safe," Carter finished finally. "I feel like she's safe here. We can keep an eye on her and make sure anyone else like Lawrence gets chased away."

Carter thought he heard something out in the hall, but when he looked that way there was nothing to see. The whole place creaked all the time, though. He was imagining things.

"Are you sure what she needs is people chasing away potential suitors?" Barnabas lifted an eyebrow.

"What does that mean?"

"It means…" Barnabas sighed. "It means the only way she'll heal is on her own. You can't do that for her. She has to be able to make her own decisions."

"I'm not trying to keep her from making her own decisions," Carter protested, but he let his head drop forward with a sigh when Barnabas raised an eyebrow in response. "Okay, maybe I'm trying to keep her from making more decisions like that one."

"Why?" Barnabas asked him. The word was mild, but there was steel there.

"Because—look what happened! He took her ship! He left her stranded on some station somewhere—"

"Where she found a job," Barnabas seemed to find that part amusing for some reason, "reached out to you, came to see you, and offered to help you take care of your children. Carter, she survived what happened to her. You need to let her stand on her own two feet. After losing someone you love…" He gave a distant smile, then turned his head as an alert sounded that Carter couldn't quite hear. "I have to go. If she leaves before I'm back, tell her I look forward to meeting her again."

"I'll make sure she stays put," Carter promised. He saw the look in Barnabas' eyes and threw his hands up. "Okay, I'll go… Ah, hell, you want me to tell her the truth, don't you? *Fine*, I'll go tell her the truth."

"Good man," Barnabas said with a smile. He cut the line, and Carter gave a sigh.

"I liked it better when my friends were cargo handlers," he groused to no one in particular. "The dregs of society didn't try to get me to be a better person." He wandered out into the hallway. "Aliana? Are you in your room?" No answer came, and he went down into the bar. "Elisa—have you seen Aliana?"

"She took something to the spaceport, I think." Elisa gave a shrug. "She said the kids were napping and she wouldn't be back before they were up."

A sense of foreboding settled over Carter. He turned without a word and took the stairs two at a time, running down the hallway to the little room they'd given to Aliana.

Her things were gone. She'd packed hastily, leaving behind a couple of shirts and a new pair of boots she'd bought since she came. Carter stared around, trying to make sense of her leaving—until he remembered the noise he'd heard in the hallway.

She'd heard everything, and he hadn't even gotten a chance to say he was sorry.

CHAPTER TWENTY-SIX

Although he had made sure to be at the conference room a few minutes ahead of schedule, Barnabas was the last to arrive. He found Shinigami standing with Gilwar, her arms crossed on her chest, studying a series of blueprints projected on the screen. Tafa was looking at an aerial surveillance shot, and Gar was paying attention to both the blueprints and the surveillance photos by turns. They were all absorbed enough in their planning that no one even noticed him enter.

He smiled as he went to lean over Tafa's and Gar's shoulders and study the map. His crew was absorbed in their work; he liked that.

Tafa gave him a nod, then used the two thumbs on one hand to point out structures on the property. "These are their water filtration systems."

Barnabas squinted at them.

"It won't be useful this time," Tafa said, "but for Jotuns, sabotage of the filtration systems would be both more vital to fix and have more of a psychological impact than it would for other species. We should keep it in mind."

"While I'm disturbed that you think we'll need to sabotage more Jotun complexes at some point, it *is* good to know." Barnabas pulled a sheet of schematics out. "I take it this is the mechanism that regulates them?"

Tafa nodded. "I'm identifying everything I can about the layout of the compound so we can see what would be the best way to go in."

Barnabas nodded and murmured his thanks before moving on to where Shinigami stood with Gilwar. There was now a schematic for a biosuit on their screen.

"These are the committee's guards," Shinigami explained to Barnabas. "Gilwar has indicated what sort of weapons they have, and where. It's probably not a complete list, but it does at least tell us what to watch out for."

Barnabas looked over the list. On the left arm of the guards' biosuits, they would have a knife, a small pistol, and a needle with some unknown poison either in or on it.

"Are the knives poisoned?" he asked Gilwar.

"Probably," Gilwar said, "but I couldn't tell you for certain. If they are, it's likely a nerve agent rather than a poison designed to kill."

"Why do you say that?"

"Poisons react very differently in different species, and not all species are consistent in the best method of poison delivery, especially if death is the goal. Not only that, size varies considerably, so it will be difficult to have enough poison to take down a Brakalon in short order. If the guards knew they would be fighting a certain species they might choose differently, but as general protocol, my guess is that they would choose a nerve agent. Nerves respond much more predictably across species, and an incapacitated enemy is one you can easily kill."

Barnabas nodded and studied the right arm. This one held a much larger gun, and the structure of the biosuit was slightly different on the opposing side to allow the biosuit to brace for recoil. Though there was no specific knife, each "finger" on the right side of the biosuit was tipped with razor-sharp serrated blades that could slide out one at a time or all at once to do damage to an opponent.

Both wrists, meanwhile, included recessed compartments with fixtures to plug the suit into various systems, presumably to hack them.

"How do Jotuns hack things?" Barnabas asked curiously.

Gilwar's head swung from side to side. "I don't...understand the question."

"Hmm. How to say this. Does the suit include fragments of code that can easily be deployed, does one Jotun hack entirely on its own, or does the hookup allow another Jotun to access the system remotely?"

"*Oh.*" Gilwar looked intrigued. "Suits include fragments of code. I hadn't considered that last option, however. That might be useful in some cases."

"Mmm." Barnabas wished he hadn't just given Jotun Intelligence a new idea for hacking, but at least Gilwar seemed to be friendly...for now. "So, what are your recommendations for an assault?"

"It will depend slightly on what Tafa says." Gilwar had

apparently familiarized himself with the crew and their areas of expertise, and Barnabas reflected that he should have expected no less from an intelligence agent.

He wondered if Gilwar had figured out yet that Shinigami was the AI who operated the ship as well as the individual inside the body.

Tafa beckoned them all over to the table and held up two fingers. "Our first thing to decide is whether or not they believe we can get onto the planet."

"They *should* assume we can," Barnabas replied after a moment's reflection. "They have to know the places we've gotten into already, don't they? Let's assume they're planning on us being there."

"Okay, so the next thing we have to guess is, are they going to place Jeltor somewhere we can get to him fairly easily and use him as bait, or do they actually want to protect him, in which case they'll have him in some version of a panic room?" Tafa looked at the rest.

No one answered for a long moment.

"It depends if they know Admiral Jeqwar declared him dead," Shinigami said finally.

"She *what?*" Gilwar demanded.

"She knows about the mind control," Barnabas explained, "and did not want to tip her hand to the whole fleet, so she told select captains that Jeltor is dead and that anyone claiming to be him, or appearing to be him is an imposter who should be killed on sight."

Gilwar nodded. "I would have expected no less from the admiral who led our fleets to victory at Jestorai."

Barnabas resolved to look up that battle at some point, although he had a fairly good idea of what Gilwar was suggesting. Admiral Jeqwar, it seemed, was well-practiced at making cold, logical decisions.

You don't want to know right now, Shinigami told him, having anticipated his desire to look it up. *You won't approve.*

Good to know, thank you.

Clever, though.

No time for that now. Focus.

She gave a small smile, and he knew she was refraining from pointing out for the hundredth time that she could focus on multiple things at once.

Fine, he grumbled, his own smile showing despite his best efforts. *Let me focus.*

She shot him a grin and sighed as she looked at the map again. "My guess is that Jeltor will be bait for us. They've had him for a while now, so they have to assume that people might have noticed him missing. If he is not what they'd hoped in terms of being their agent, it might make sense to use him to take us out."

"Then they'll be in the main house," Tafa predicted. "There's an entertaining area, sunken, easy to flood if the guests are Jotuns, easy to keep dry if the guests are some other species. It's very elegant, very…show-off-y?"

"Ostentatious?" Barnabas suggested.

"Sure." Tafa shrugged.

You're ostentatious, Shinigami accused. *With your fancy words.*

With my correct *words?*

She rolled her eyes.

"If he's meant to be bait," Gilwar said, "and Grisor wants to show off—which is, I think, what Tafa was suggesting, yes? Yes, then he will likely flood the area when we're there. Most Jotuns believe their species is superior to others, and in someone like Grisor, that opinion is almost an obsession. He'll want to do something to you that a Jotun could survive but you won't be able to."

"And he doesn't know what we are," Shinigami said smugly. "Gar, you can breathe underwater, right?"

"It's not comfortable, and I can't do it for a huge amount of time," Gar said, "but for the length of a fight, yes. Enough to surprise them certainly, unless they're very well versed in Luvendi physiology."

"They're not," Gilwar said. "They haven't bothered with the Luvendi so far." He looked at them curiously. "So you actually think this is worth trying?"

"Yes," Barnabas said at the same time as Shinigami, Gar, and Tafa.

If Gilwar had had eyebrows, Barnabas assumed they would have shot up in surprise. As it was, there was merely a pause before the mechanical head nodded.

"I say we go in pretending to bargain," Shinigami said. "We can have the ship on standby in case we need it—"

"Is this a flamethrower plan?" Barnabas interrupted.

"You have to ask? Yes, *obviously* it is a flamethrower plan. They're bringing the water, we're bringing the fire. Meanwhile, we sneak Gilwar off the ship somehow to get into their systems and mess with them. Too bad he doesn't have a suit like the assassin, huh?"

"Kantar?" Gilwar asked. When everyone looked at him, he gave a discreet mechanical cough. "I did not realize you did not know her name. I regret telling her not to explain things to you."

"*You* hired her?" Barnabas asked. Somewhat annoyed, he added, "And, yes, it would have been helpful to have more knowledge about what was going on."

"We had hoped not to involve other species," Gilwar explained. It was impossible to tell from his tone whether he regretted his actions. "You're very determined, however, even though this isn't your sector."

"My sector?" Barnabas gave him a look.

"*Our* sector," Shinigami corrected helpfully. She gave him a bland smile when he rolled his eyes and laughed.

"I see no particular human interest in this," Gilwar said. "Rather, I see no reason they would intervene in the particular way that they have."

"I'm not a human emissary," Barnabas explained. "I'm a Ranger."

"A vigilante," Shinigami said after a pause. "He goes wherever there is injustice and rights things for their own sake, not for *human interests.*"

"Ah." Again, it was impossible to tell what Gilwar thought from his tone. Even his thoughts were very calm when Barnabas probed them lightly. "A justiciar."

"As good a term as any, I suppose." Barnabas nodded to the group. "Everyone get ready. Shinigami, you didn't mention the satellites. Do you think you can get back through those?"

"I do." She followed him out the door and along the corridor. "I'm basing my strategy on the Ubuara hive-mind thing they have going on. I started to come up with the idea when we were getting through the turrets on the way to the laboratory. I won't be doing a hard hack of any of the systems, I'll be having each satellite influence its neighbors to be focusing elsewhere using different amounts of force; all that."

"I like that." Barnabas grinned.

"I thought you might. It has your trademark sneakiness, and we *do* have a reputation to uphold, you know." She followed him into his quarters.

"Can I help you?" Barnabas knew she was not human and that she could see into his room at all times if she wished to do so, but it still felt strange to consider changing in front of her when she was standing right here in a human-looking body.

She must have guessed what he was thinking because she snorted. "I'll look the other way," she offered, then turned around and studied the ceiling.

"Thank you." Barnabas shook his head and began to change, laying his clothes neatly on the bed for him to hang up. The ship would do it for him if he wanted, of course, but he believed that habits of neatness were valuable.

This was the sort of sentiment that made Shinigami tell him he was boring at parties. The thought made him smile as he looked at her back. "Was there something you wanted to talk to me about?"

"Yes, actually." She instinctively turned back toward him before checking herself and looking at the ceiling again. "Are you all right?"

Barnabas paused in the process of pulling his light-weight undershirt on. With reinforced fibers and the team's trademark attention to detail, it was not only comfortable but also strong enough to repel most knives. It added a valuable layer between his skin and his armor.

He sat on the bed and considered. "I feel steadier."

"You *seem* steadier. Can I turn around now?"

"Yes." Barnabas smiled slightly and met her eyes. "Having you here, knowing that you wouldn't let me go over the edge—I hadn't even considered it, but I must have known on some level that it was a possibility. Your offer helped more than you know." He considered. "And then I spoke to Carter, and I realized something else."

Shinigami waited, head cocked to the side curiously.

"Catherine," Barnabas said, by way of explanation. "I watched her slip away. I watched her turn into a different person. I couldn't stop any of it. To see that happen to Jeltor, maybe to millions of others…it's horrifying."

Shinigami hesitated. "You know they won't manage it, right?" she said finally. "We'll stop them."

Barnabas looked at her. They might already be too late, and he had to accept that. To his surprise, telling himself that seemed to make it better, rather than not quite thinking it or not letting himself think it. "Shinigami, what if they've turned Jeltor? What if he's loyal to Grisor now above all else?"

"Then we kill Grisor." Shinigami shrugged. "Problem solved."

Barnabas gave a bark of laughter and dropped his face into his hands for a moment. His shoulders shook with mirth. "Oh, Shinigami, what would I do without you?"

"Solve problems the boring way," Shinigami told him promptly. "Come on, let's go. We're almost on the surface."

"*What? You— What?*"

"I didn't want to bother you with the trivial bits. It turns out the Jotun systems are very strong against a hard hack but very, very weak against gentle persuasion." She looked immensely pleased with herself. "I'm going to go get my weapons!"

Barnabas stared after her for a moment, then finished dressing, still chuckling. He was sure he'd do just fine without Shinigami and the rest of his crew.

But his life *definitely* wouldn't be as much fun.

CHAPTER TWENTY-SEVEN

It was quiet as the *Shinigami* made its way down to the surface. In fact, it was far *too* quiet. Barnabas, leaning against the wall next to the airlock, wondered if he should ask if the satellites had been turned off, but Shinigami anticipated the question.

"I really did fool them," she told him. There was a note of wounded pride in her voice. "They'll probably change those specific protocols in the future, but changing all of their systems won't be so easy."

Gar had joined them. "Maybe they don't know we're here—or they haven't had as much warning as they expected. You know, like they thought they would see a certain number of explosions or missile launches or something, and that would be their cue to prepare."

The ship gave a small shudder.

"Like that?" Barnabas asked.

"That," Shinigami said with satisfaction, "was Gilwar being launched out of a missile tube."

Barnabas froze, and Gar made a small worried noise.

"He *asked* me to," Shinigami clarified. "You two are so suspicious. He knows what he's doing. Well, he seems to. I didn't see any signs that he was lying. I don't think he knows that I can read Jotun emotions."

"We're still waiting for your master class on that, by the way," Barnabas told her. "Time to hope he can get something useful done, I suppose."

"Mmhmm." She checked her weapons one last time. "Do you think *I* could get guns embedded in my arms?" she asked wistfully.

"Let's say no."

"Oh, come on, you didn't think about that at all."

"A biosuit is much bulkier than you are," Barnabas said, scrambling for a plausible-sounding reason. "You couldn't get those guns in there without it being obvious."

"On the plus side, I could actually be talking about *guns* when I said 'these guns.'"

"I…" Barnabas looked at the ceiling and tried to figure out where to go from here.

"I'll talk to Jean about it."

"Please don't. I'm not sure I'm ready to have an associate with embedded guns."

"So you *do* think it's possible!" Shinigami looked triumphant.

Barnabas knew he needed to change the subject before she asked about embedding a flamethrower. "All right. Tafa…there you are. You'll be ready for our signal when we need extraction, yes?"

Tafa nodded. "And I'll let you know if I see anything on the scanners that looks hinky." She had recently started watching human movies and was surprisingly good at learning colloquialisms. "Hinky" was one of her favorites thus far.

"Right." Barnabas nodded to Gar and Shinigami. "So we go in and pretend to be bargaining to get Jeltor back."

"And you have an idea of how to convince them you're *not* there to burn the place to the ground?" Shinigami asked skeptically.

"Sort of. The fact that I haven't yet burned it to the ground seems like a good place to start." Barnabas gave them all a smile and, as the blast doors opened, turned and walked down the gangway.

It was paradise—that was his first thought. The air seemed to be the perfect temperature, the wind was rustling in the abundant greenery, and there was the pleasant smell of sea, flowers, and fresh air. Grisor had made the most of this place, enhancing the natural landscape with faint touches of technology.

A man of taste. Barnabas suspected that Tafa and Gilwar were right that Grisor's pride was heavily invested in his self-image of being a civilized and refined person. That would be his weakness, and Barnabas hoped to exploit it.

It looked like he would have the opportunity to try immediately, given that Grisor was waiting for them. Two absolutely massive bodyguards flanked him, their suits bristling with far more weapons than Gilwar's schematics had shown. Between them, Grisor looked slender and graceful.

"Barnabas." His voice was warm and rich. Well-suited, Barnabas guessed, to making allies in private talks or stirring emotion with speeches in the Senate. "We meet in person at last." He sounded delighted, except for the very faint undercurrent of cruelty in his voice.

Barnabas decided to play the same game. He'd known Michael's son David, after all. This was hardly anything new to him. He smiled back and went over to hold out his hand. He was risking immediate assassination, of course…

If they could summon enough force to kill him in one strike. He doubted they could.

"Senator Grisor." He filled his voice with just as much warmth and shook the Jotun's hand. "Thank you for meeting with me. I'm glad we could do this without…unpleasantness."

Grisor laughed heartily. He turned and Barnabas fell in beside him, strolling along with the bodyguards on one side and Shinigami and Gar on the other. Both Shinigami and Gar were wearing masks that obscured their features, so it was impossible to be certain of Gar's species.

"There is no need for unpleasantness," Grisor said as they walked. "I am not a soldier, to solve every problem with ships and guns." Deep contempt showed for just a moment, and Barnabas heard his hatred of the Navy and their meddling. "Tell me, what did you wish to discuss?"

"Ah." Barnabas tilted his face to the sky and studied it for a moment. *Shinigami, you and Gar pick out which guards you're going to neutralize.*

On it, boss.

"It is a small matter, in some respects," Barnabas said. "But perhaps one that a man of your moral code would be unwilling to compromise on."

Grisor said nothing. His face was turned toward Barnabas expectantly as the group made their slow way down a broad avenue lined with flowering trees toward the amphitheater Tafa had described.

"I understand you were wronged by a friend of mine," Barnabas said. "He has…damaged your interests, or at least potentially done so. I gather you've brought him here to even the score. I know it is a great deal to ask since there is a need to make an example, but I hoped we might come to a mutually beneficial agreement that resulted in his release. Any…*damage*…done to him would, of course, be water under the bridge."

You're disturbingly good at that, Shinigami commented.

Agreed, Gar said.

I'm not enjoying it. Barnabas didn't look at them. *But the payoff should be good.*

Grisor said nothing for a moment. "I must admit, from your reputation, I didn't expect this attitude."

Barnabas gave a laugh. "Like you, I must sometimes make an example. What man of principle does not need to do so?"

Grisor made a small sound that might have been agreement. Barnabas, having met quite a few politicians, understood it to be a good tactic for not being caught on record giving any sort of strong opinion.

"So," the Jotun said finally, "what are you offering?"

"*Ah.*" Barnabas let his smile broaden. "I think you will like this," he said as if confiding a secret. He chose his words carefully. "It should serve your interests and repair the damage that has been done."

"I'm intrigued." Grisor sounded cautiously optimistic.

"I hoped you would say that." They had reached the

amphitheater and Barnabas looked at it with a jaded eye. It was beautiful, of course, but he had seen enough people like Grisor to know exactly what types of ugliness lurked beneath the surface of this place: slavery, torture, control, and cruelty.

Get ready.

Aye-aye.

Barnabas turned his head to look at Grisor. He was, rather ostentatiously, not in a battle stance. He had linked his hands behind his back and did not turn his body toward his opponent. A fight began long before blows were exchanged in the subtle cues that drew an enemy's eye...or induced one to pass over, unseen.

"I will give you," Barnabas said, "and *every* member of the Infrastructure Revitalization Committee, a clean and painless death. I will raze all mention of your existence from the official record, so only your associates know about the cancer that lurked within their society."

At his side, Grisor went still.

"This is a sacrifice, you understand." Barnabas kept his tone light. "The families of the aliens you abducted and tortured should know what happened. The rest of the species in this sector should know. But I am willing, for the sake of the citizens you wish to raise up, to let this be a secret. Instead of a disgrace, a curse, a footnote in history whose name is spoken with contempt, you and your colleagues will merely be forgotten."

He met the eyes of Grisor's mechanical face and smiled. It was not a kind smile, and it was not the face of blind Justice. It was the face of a man who saw, measured, and chose.

"You will—" Grisor began.

"Die" had probably been the end of that statement, but Barnabas didn't care. His fist shot out sideways and embedded his knife, to the hilt, in the hip of Grisor's suit.

Gar and Shinigami had chosen their targets, but they weren't quite as quick off the mark as Barnabas was. They launched into motion, Gar just a split-second behind the guards, Shinigami recovering from her lapse with the superhuman speed she'd been built to have. An explosive round caught the more distant guard in the head, and it was knocked, heavy and awkward, off-balance.

Barnabas didn't wait to see how the fight behind him would play out. He wrenched Grisor off balance, swung him in a wide arc, and gave a heavy kick to send the Jotun tumbling down the steps of the amphitheater. He felt a single moment of satisfaction.

Tafa and Shinigami yelled through the Etheric at the same time, and the potted plants at the base and rim of the amphitheater popped up to reveal turrets.

Barnabas swore and threw himself down the stairs after Grisor. *Gar! Get to cover!*

I'm handling it! Shinigami called. *I just need to get to the controls. Tafa—*

Gilwar says he's on it, Tafa reported. *Just hold out!*

Behind him, Barnabas heard Gar give his ridiculous battle cry and turned in time to watch Gar vault into the air, climb the back of a guard's suit, and begin working on the weak points near the sensor array, ducking out of the way of the guard's weapons-heavy arms.

Shinigami, not content to sit by while Gilwar did his work, was lobbing grenades and firing explosive rounds by turn, creating dead zones by taking some of the turrets out of the mix. Barnabas couldn't see the pattern she was using, but he was sure there was one.

There was no time to waste. He landed near Grisor on the floor of the amphitheater, rolled to his feet, and dragged the senator toward the door that led into the building. A few steps, a few more—

Grisor was now between Barnabas and the turrets. He snarled and fought, but his suit wasn't as strong as the guards' suits, and Barnabas was continuing to keep him off-balance.

"So," Barnabas said pleasantly, "do we have a deal?"

The shot took him fully in the back, sending him staggering forward. Barnabas felt the breath go out of his lungs and his armor, as advanced as it was, could not keep his ribs from breaking and several organs from rupturing. He let go of Grisor as red haze covered his vision. He just had to survive while his body repaired itself—

"No," Jeltor called. He stepped into the light of the amphitheater, a new suit gleaming over his body, a smoking gun leveled at Barnabas. "We don't have a deal."

CHAPTER TWENTY-EIGHT

Take out the suit! Shinigami's yell echoed in Barnabas' head. *Now! We'll take the guards. Get the* suit!

Barnabas was already moving before he realized how deeply he'd come to trust Shinigami. He hadn't even hesitated before taking her suggestion. If anyone had asked him, however, he would have said that—outside of a battle situation with an established chain of command—he could not imagine responding this way to anyone other than Bethany Anne. Things had changed.

For the better.

His bones and organs healed more every second as he threw himself at Jeltor.

Jeltor, forgive me. I'm sorry. He grabbed for the arms of the suit, intending to wrench one of them off. He would disable the suit piece by piece.

Or...that was the plan. Jeltor, however, directed a hard punch at Barnabas' still-healing body, stepping inside the range of his arms. One mechanical hand grabbed Barnabas' throat and squeezed.

"You will not hurt His Excellency," Jeltor commanded.

Somewhere nearby, Grisor was laughing. Barnabas could hear it as the nanites began their work anew and his mind reeled from the pain. He could not let Jeltor crush his throat, but to strike at the tank would be to kill his friend—and he was not going to do that. He clung to Jeltor's arm and looked into the tank.

"You're still Jeltor," he wheezed to the Jotun floating in there. "They burned this into you with pain and mind games, but you're still *Jeltor*. The part of you that knows what Grisor is—that part is still there. They can tell you to be loyal to him, but they can't make the whole rest of your mind agree. He's going against everything you stand for."

Jeltor hit him again, and there was the searing pain of ribs cracking a second time.

Barnabas! Shinigami's scream seemed to echo in his ears as well as his mind, and then he realized she truly *had* yelled it aloud, using it as a battle cry while she broke one of the guards in two and tossed his body down the stairs, fluid pooling and draining away from the limp Jotun body inside. *Get out of there first,* then *try to get into his head!*

Barnabas swung into action at once, grabbing for a knife and electrifying it before he plunged it into Jeltor's wrist. The biosuit jerked, power ricocheting through the internal circuits, and Barnabas stumbled away. He saw Grisor waiting and ran the other way, heedless of the laughter.

You think I'm defeated? he thought savagely. *You have no idea what you're in for.* With each passing second he stood outside Jeltor's range he was healing.

Four shots echoed nearby in such close succession that they must have come from multiple guns. Barnabas looked that way, a hand still pressed to his ribs, and saw both Shinigami and Gar pointing their smoking weapons at the husk of the last guard.

The turrets had been swiveling, unsure of their targets with so many of their own in the mix, but now they centered on Shinigami and Gar without hesitation.

"Down!" Barnabas yelled. The acoustics were so good that his call was deafening. It rolled through the space long after Shinigami and Gar had hit the floor on the top level of the amphitheater and crawled to shelter behind some of the top turrets.

Tafa, what's Gilwar's status on the turrets?

He says he's close.

They're shooting at us! Barnabas dove behind shallow cover and lobbed a grenade at the turret closest to him. *Tell him to hurry it up!*

With a whine and a defeated sigh, the turrets stopped firing and dropped gracelessly back down. Several of the potted plants, jostled a bit too much, tipped onto the ground. It was almost enough to make Barnabas laugh—until he heard the trickling sound of water.

Sonofa—every damned time with these people.

To be fair, they are *an aquatic species.*

That will be enough out of you. Laughing helped, now that his internal organs were fixed. Barnabas stood, his mind made up and his fingers ready to grab for his Jean Dukes.

He had to keep joking, or he would realize how high the stakes were.

"Jeltor."

A hollow boom sounded as the gun in Jeltor's arm went off. This time, however, Barnabas had anticipated it. The round passed harmlessly through empty air and made a smoking dent in the wall behind him.

Barnabas, meanwhile, took shelter behind a nearby potted plant.

"Jeltor, you said you once believed that Jotuns were superior to all other species. That belief did not survive when you started to meet other aliens."

"Come out." Jeltor sounded frustrated. "Barnabas, this isn't funny. You came here and tried to kill His Excellency. You want to destroy the Jotun people, give us a slow death you can pretend you have no knowledge of while other species cause chaos across the sector."

"Why would I want that?" Barnabas asked calmly.

"Because your Federation wants us to be too concerned with each other to hurt them!" Jeltor called back. "They know that if we joined together, they could be wiped off the map."

"Jeltor, I assure you that is not—" Barnabas paused. "You know me," he said. "You've watched me take actions that would *not* expose your species to—"

Left! Go!

Again, Barnabas listened without hesitation, and he was glad he had done so when the stone base of the potted plant exploded into chunks of flaming rubble.

Dear God, what kind of ammunition does he have?

The really fun kind. I mean, if you're shooting it. Less so if you're the one having to get out of the way.

Noticed that, did you? Barnabas listened to the heavy steps coming closer, formulated his plan in a split-second, and hurtled out of cover in silence and with deadly speed. His enhanced strength sent him far higher into the air when he leapt than Jeltor expected, and as shots peppered the air, Barnabas came down on Jeltor's head and chest, releasing bots onto the suit and punching the sensor array. *Shinigami, what can you do with those?*

I'll let you know when I have something. Plan as if there's nothing I can do.

Barnabas sent back a wordless assent and slammed his fist down three more times into the visual sensor display. Unless he was very much mistaken, this now gave him two large blind spots on Jeltor's sides, where there was always armor plating, and would make even front and back vision more difficult for his opponent.

He jumped free and landed lightly on the ground, circling to stay in the blind spot as Jeltor staggered in a circle, looking for him.

"Jeltor, you know that what Grisor offers is false security," Barnabas warned. "He can't ever give you a peaceful world. A world that is built on violence and cruelty will always be cruel. He will not become kind once he has all of you in his thrall. No, he'll use that to silence dissent while he and his friends grow rich and powerful."

"Liar!" Jeltor called. He sounded furious.

"Don't listen to him, Jeltor." Grisor sounded soothing and utterly calm, as though he were not at all afraid. "Remember the fear of your past life? Remember the insecurity, the failure? You will never have to fear that again. No other species will threaten us."

"Jeltor, if what he offers you is so wonderful, why hasn't *he* undergone the procedure?" Barnabas locked eyes with Grisor. *I'm coming for you, you bastard.*

"For the one who rises to lead, there cannot be any procedure." Grisor was beginning to sound panicked. "I am fully devoted to my ideals already. I seek only to give others the peace I already have."

"Does he sound peaceful, Jeltor? Does he sound like he's free from fear?"

Jeltor gave a mechanical sound, half-groan and half-shriek.

The suit keeps frying the bots, Shinigami reported, frustrated. *They must be used to this as a form of sabotage. I have one more, but—dammit! No more. I can't help. I'm sorry, but you're doing well. You're sowing seeds of doubt.*

Thank you. Barnabas darted through Jeltor's field of vision, hoping to draw his attention, and the gun did indeed come up to follow him. It was slow, however, tracking based on Jeltor's warped perception of a world part aquatic and part air. *I know what I have to do, then.*

He took two steps and jumped once more, but this time he went even higher, leaping entirely over Jeltor's hulking new biosuit and landing with crushing force on Grisor.

Heyyyyy, you listened!

Yeah, yeah, don't make a big thing of it. Barnabas ripped an arm free before Grisor could recover and dragged the senator off-balance once more. The water was finally beginning to fill the amphitheater, rising very slowly. *Is Gilwar interfering with the water?*

He says he is, Tafa said. *He shut off all but one of the filtration plants, and the system is designed not to use water that's unclean because the Jotuns would be swimming in it.*

Clever. Barnabas smiled as he held his knife to the gap between Grisor's armor plating. *So it came in useful after all. Good call, Tafa.*

To Jeltor, he called, "Over here."

Whoa, wait! Shinigami sounded angry. *You're not just killing Grisor?*

Trust me.

She grumbled.

Jeltor turned and froze.

"Jeltor, you remember who you were," Barnabas exclaimed desperately. This wasn't like it had been with Catherine, he told himself. Catherine's mind had been destroyed. Jeltor's had merely been changed. It could be changed back.

Jeltor said nothing, keeping his arm leveled at Barnabas uncertainly. He could not shoot at Grisor; it went against all his programming, and that programming went deep.

Please, Barnabas whispered to Jeltor. He did not know if Jeltor could hear him anymore, but he had to try. *This isn't you.*

And then his ear caught the very faint sound of the door opening. It was meant to be silent, but Barnabas wasn't a normal being, and he had already nearly been killed by that same trick today. He whirled, his Jean Dukes coming up as he fired three times. The sound of shots from nearby told him that Shinigami and Gar had done the same thing.

It was the last guard from the laboratory, staggering

back with his suit shattered. For a moment, Barnabas could feel the Jotun's rage for his lost team members, and there was an unexpected wave of sympathy—

The splashing behind him told him to refocus his attention. He whirled, and found Jeltor ushering Grisor to safety.

"Jeltor! Think about this! Think! Think for yourself!" Barnabas could hear the terror in his own words. "Remember who you *are*, not who they told you to be."

"Stay away." Jeltor pointed his gun at Barnabas.

"Shoot him!" Grisor yelled.

Barnabas did the only thing he could think of. He put his hands up and looked at Jeltor through the wall of the tank. "Jeltor, it's me. I don't want to hurt you. I *won't* hurt you."

"Jeltor, *shoot* him!"

Jeltor stood frozen, indecision plain on his features. Then, with a shriek of anguish, he fired. He turned and pushed Grisor through a hidden door, moving more quickly than Barnabas would have believed possible.

"Jeltor!"

But Jeltor was gone, doors slamming closed across the base.

Shinigami had used her scanners, and now she said gravely, *We're not getting in there—and there are guards mobilizing.*

But we have to—

We'll come back for him. Barnabas, he... Her voice trailed off. When Barnabas looked up, she was staring at him, clearly hating what she was saying.

He fired, Gar said, *but he didn't shoot to kill. He didn't even shoot to wound.*

He's still in there. Barnabas took two steps toward the door.

And he chose Grisor—for now. Barnabas, remember what you told him: his view of the Jotuns didn't survive reality. You have to trust that it will happen again.

When he said nothing, Shinigami added softly, *You told me I could call the shots on this one when I needed to. I need to now. We'll get him back, but this isn't the way.*

Barnabas closed his eyes, dropping his head into one hand for a moment before he nodded. He went up the stairs wordlessly with the sound of the *Shinigami's* engines coming closer and the distant sounds of gunfire.

"Where's Gilwar?" he asked.

Shinigami pointed. On the open gangway of the *Shinigami*, Gilwar was waiting to help them aboard. Barnabas ushered Gar and Shinigami ahead of him and then leapt aboard himself, running down the slope of the gangway as it closed.

"Good to see you safe," he told Gilwar.

"And you," Gilwar said. "I saw what happened." His face might not hold expressions, but the meaning could not be mistaken: *it happened, you didn't imagine it.*

"We're going to get him back," Barnabas told all of them. "We're going to get him back, and we're going to give Justice to those they've hurt."

"You promised Grisor a painless death," Shinigami said. She did not sound disapproving, only interested. "Was it a lie?"

"It wasn't a lie." Barnabas met her eyes. "If he had

251

agreed and returned Jeltor to me, I would have done it. It wouldn't have sat easily with me, but for the sake of the Jotun people, I could have done it. I wouldn't have offered if I couldn't, not with honor at stake."

Shinigami was beginning to smile. "But?"

Barnabas smiled back and felt the coldness of it down to his bones.

"But he *didn't* take the offer, did he?"

EPILOGUE

The station they stopped at was so small that it wasn't even named, but Barnabas' golden rule still held true: it didn't matter how far you went or how remote you were, if there were multiple people living there and others passing through, there was *going* to be a bar.

Barnabas held up his glass, and the others followed suit —with the exception of Gilwar, of course, who held up an empty hand.

"To Jeltor," Barnabas said softly. "To our friend, who is still inside. Who can be brought back."

Shinigami lifted the liquid to her lips. While she couldn't technically take sustenance from substances, she *could* ingest them and analyze them. She stopped when Barnabas shook his head slightly.

"I wasn't quite finished. To my friends, who look out for each other. Who go into danger without complaint because there are those who depend on them...and who speak the truth to me when I need to hear it." He held his glass out to clink it against each of theirs and tap it against Gilwar's fingers, and then he drank. "This stuff is truly vile."

"I'm not sure it's meant to be ingestible," Shinigami said doubtfully, staring down into the glass. "The chemical composition is remarkably close to poison."

"Alcohol *is* poison," Gar informed her cheerfully. "Drink up."

Shinigami laughed and clinked glasses with him, and Barnabas sat back to watch the four of them as they spoke and laughed. Gilwar was discussing the layout of senatorial compounds with Tafa, and Gar and Shinigami were having a drinking contest—slightly unfair, in Barnabas' opinion. The rest of the bar was oblivious to his group.

He looked down into his cup with a small smile.

Hey, boss. Shinigami caught his eye when he looked up. *Where's Gar?*

Getting another round. She smiled. *What are you thinking about?*

Chess. Barnabas saw her smile and shook his head. *Not... like that.* He sighed as he looked around, then leaned on the table and considered. *Chess is supposed to teach you tactics, but chess pieces don't have souls or lives—or families. You never have to worry about your opponent's pawns, just about killing their king.*

Shinigami said nothing, watching him quietly.

I promised Grisor I would let this be forgotten because part of me thinks it's the right thing to do, Barnabas said. *The Jotun people had nothing to do with this. They don't deserve to suffer for it if someone tries to turn it into a war.*

But?

But smoothing it over and pretending it never happened means it might happen again. Barnabas took a gulp of his drink and choked. *I forgot I shouldn't be drinking that.*

Shinigami grinned as she pounded him on the back. *Breathe,* she advised. *Right, good. Now drink the rest while you're still numb. Now, now,* now!

Barnabas downed the rest of it and made a pained whimpering noise. *Oh, God, that was disgusting. It hurts. I regret drinking that. Why did I listen to you?*

Because it's fun. I told Gar to get you a drink, too. She nodded to where Gar was making his way back from the bar with three drinks. *Come on, let's get soused and sing embarrassing songs about honor and friendship.*

Barnabas laughed. Beyond this station was a committee hellbent on destruction, with a pawn they had brainwashed into helping them. There was a war brewing that could destroy most of the sector if he let it.

He didn't intend to let it.

But before he stopped it, he would let his team relax a bit. He took a glass from Gar, reminded himself that pain was an excellent teacher, and drank it in one go. When Shinigami and Gar finished their drinks, Barnabas was laughing.

"What?" Gar was already loopy.

"Pain is an excellent teacher," Barnabas got out between whoops of laughter. "It's supposed to teach you *not* to do things, though."

"What's your point?" Shinigami raised an eyebrow.

"My point is that we're being remarkably stupid, and I'm quite enjoying it." Barnabas stood. He caught a flicker out of the corner of his eye and looked out into the hallway, but saw nothing. Shaking his head to clear it, he picked up the empty glasses with a smile. "Next round's on me."

Aliana turned the corner and kept walking, her heart pounding. He'd almost seen her; she was sure of it. It was like he'd felt her watching him.

She supposed he was the one who'd looked over, not the one with the double-pupiled eyes or the woman. Carter had said she was an AI. Both of those people frightened her a little. Barnabas, though…

She shook her head slightly.

"Aliana." Zinqued was waiting at the ship, his arms spread wide. "You took a while getting here. I thought you might not be coming."

"And I *hoped* you wouldn't," Tik'ta agreed, but Aliana heard fondness in her tone.

"You *did* get my message, right?" Aliana frowned at them. "I don't think it can be done. I don't think the *Shinigami* can be stolen—and I'm not sure I want to. The things he's doing are important."

"He'll do them either way," Zinqued said confidently. "And you'll find a way to steal the ship. I'm sure of it." He stepped back and held out an arm, welcoming her onto the ship. "I'm curious, though. What made you decide to come back?"

"I'm also curious," Tik'ta chimed in as she followed them.

Aliana paused inside the ship, deciding how much

to say.

"I thought I could run away from my problems," she said finally. "That mistakes could just be forgotten, and I could rely on someone else to pick me up and dust me off. But I can't. Until I've gotten even with Lawrence and made him pay for what he did, I can't forget it. It will eat at me."

She ducked her head and made for her cabin before they could ask her anything more. She didn't want to answer their questions any more than she wanted to answer her uncle's. He had sent her a worried message after she left, and she still had not responded.

Now, though, she slumped onto the tiny cot and typed out a brief reply: *I need to do this. Tell Elisa and the kids I love them. I miss you guys already.*

She did, after all. She missed the creaky apartment over the bar. She missed the bar. She missed Carter and Elisa and the twins. She even missed the new baby, although she hadn't met it yet.

But she didn't belong there. She never had, even though Carter had wanted her to stay. She still hadn't gotten her life together—and she was determined not to be anyone's charity case. She wiped the tears off her cheeks, lifted her chin, and set about unpacking.

She was going to make Lawrence pay.

———

Cries of pain echoed off the walls as Grisor paced.

Six guards had been lost, not to mention the laboratory, the data, and the robotic army Biset had foolishly sacrificed—ah, yes, and the remnants of the Yennai fleet. It was good for Biset's sake that he was dead. Grisor would not have given him as quick and clean a death as Barnabas had.

Now...

Now there was very little time.

Grisor went to the door and stared into the tank. Jeltor should have obeyed him at once when ordered to shoot. It was troubling that he had not, and without the research team to innovate, Grisor was not certain if any modifications should be made to the program.

He resolved not to think of those issues just yet. If it worked, he would only have wasted his time. If it did not work, *then* he would worry.

In the meantime, he strode to a screen and brought up a sector map. His fingers hovered over a few of the shining dots as he considered. They had to begin their plan now. Once the admirals were converted—and they *would* be—they must be ready to swing into action at once.

Which alien race to bring into the fold first? That was the only question.

Grisor's fingers hovered for a moment longer, then tapped a binary star system. The planet that came up on the screen was a mix of lush vegetation and wasteland. It was battered by storms, famously harsh, and the aliens it had produced were almost as terrifying.

Yes. The Brakalons would be a good first addition to the committee's forces.

FINIS

Thank you for following Barnabas's story! I don't know if anyone's let you in on this secret yet, but writing a series is often just as surprising as reading one. We know some of what's coming down the pike, of course, but seeing it unfold is a revelation every time. Even though I already begin each series with anticipation, looking forward to spending all that time with the characters, that is nothing compared to how much I care for them by the end of the series.

We've seen Barnabas come farther than I think he would have thought possible, from someone who still had not processed his grief about Catherine, to someone who is willing to rely on his friends. Shinigami's evolution has been just as surprising to her. Humans are definitely a force of chaos!

As always, I want to thank Michael, first and foremost, for bringing me on board and letting me work with him on this series. I loved Barnabas since he first showed up and was so lucky to get to be a part of this story! My beta readers, both the JIT group and the crew who bravely take the bullet of looking at my rough drafts, have been amazing as well, as has the editorial and administrative team that makes LMBPN run so smoothly! Thanks to Craig, also, for allowing Bustamove in for a cameo.

To the readers - I love your energy, your passion for this universe, and the way you support all of us involved in the KGU. Thank you so, so, so much. There's more Barnabas on the way, but I know how much you all read! If you're looking for something new in the meantime, I suggest The Dragon Corps (seven books and counting!) and Bound Sorcery (the fourth book in the Shadows of Magic series will be out soon).

Last but not least, I want to thank my own adorable ball of chaos, L, who is teaching me so much every day about how to appreciate everything I have, and how to see the world with new eyes.

Until next time,
Nat

OCTOBER 31, 2018

THANK YOU for not only reading this story, but these author notes as well .

RANDOM (*sometimes*) THOUGHTS?

I know, this is a really random thought that without context (which is too personal to share) remember that family and friends might not be ignoring you. They might just have busy lives and while you are important, it slipped their mind as they have had to deal with the here and now for too long..

They love you. Just pick up the phone and chat with them sometime.

(Barring that support – pick up and read another LMBPN book – it might not help a relationship, but at least it should be fun.)

HOW TO MARKET FOR BOOKS YOU LOVE

We are able to support our efforts with you reading our books and we appreciate you doing this!

If you enjoyed this or ANY book by any author, especially Indie published, we always appreciate if you make the time to review a book, as it lets other readers who might be on the fence to take a chance on it as well.

AROUND THE WORLD IN 80 DAYS (rather, where am I writing these and what is going on?)

One of the interesting (at least for me) aspects of my life is the ability to work from anywhere and at anytime. In the future, I hope to re-read my own author notes and remember my life as a diary entry.

For these author notes I am sitting in the London Hotel – West Hollywood which is one block (barely) away from the Whisky a Go-Go club for concerts.

My ears are ringing which is a common occurrence when you listen to music too loud for too long. My younger brother (well, he is 42) and I went to go see the band Stryper who was playing at the Whisky on Halloween night and I have to say, it was a *blast*.

I've followed this band since high school, and I have probably seen them play in concert about seven times in my life.

I say about because time for me is murky. I can dream up new stuff into the future all day long. Ask me what I had for lunch last Wednesday (or how many times I have seen a band play over the last 35 or so years) and I'm a bit vague on that information.

For making a business run on fictional stories, this

forward looking creative brain is a superpower. For helping me to remember important events which need to be celebrated with certain people? It is a millstone around my neck. Normally, I celebrate my brain. When I'm in the relationship doghouse, not so much.

FAN PRICING

If you would like to find out what LMBPN is doing, and the books we are publishing, just sign up at http://lmbpn.com/email/ . When you sign up, we notify you of books coming out for the week, any new posts of interest in the books and pop culture arena and the fan pricing on Saturday.

Ad Aeternitatem,
Michael Anderle

BOOKS BY NATALIE GREY

Shadows of Magic

Bound Sorcery

Blood Sorcery

Bright Sorcery

Set in the Kurtherian Gambit Universe

Bellatrix

Challenges

Risk Be Damned

Damned to Hell

Vigilante

Sentinel

Warden

Paladin

Justiciar

Defender

Writing as Moira Katson

Shadowborn

Shadowforged

Shadow's End

Daughter of Ashes

Mahalia

CONNECT WITH THE AUTHORS

Natalie Grey Social

Email List

https://landing.mailerlite.com/webforms/landing/w0k9j4

Follow Natalie on Amazon

https://www.amazon.com/Natalie-Grey/e/B01MYG7K8P/

Facebook

https://www.facebook.com/Natalie-Grey-393234677682987/

Michael Anderle Social

Website: http://lmbpn.com

Email List: http://lmbpn.com/email/

Facebook:
www.facebook.com/TheKurtherianGambitBooks